DIRTY TALKER

PIPER RAYNE

Cover design: MadHat Covers

Model: Zack Salaun

Photographer: Wander Aguilar

Line Editor: Love N Books

Proof Reader: Shawna Gavas, Behind The Writer

About Dirty Talker

Turn-ons...

Party girls.
Platinum blondes.
Zero expectations.

I used to think that if you could combine all three into one female, you'd have the perfect woman.

Then why the hell does Ava Pearson—an outdoorsy girl, a brunette, and a woman who screams stability and responsibility—seem to be the only woman on my mind lately?

I've got enough obligations without adding any complications to the mix—my son, my bar...well, that's about it. But that's enough for a guy like me.

It's the cupcakes. It's gotta be the cupcakes she bakes that keep me coming back for more. The way to a man's heart is through his stomach, right? Apparently, it's a direct target to his junk, too.

Did I forget to mention that she's my buddy's daughter... another member of the Single Dads Club's daughter?

Ava might say she can handle being friends-with-benefits, but I'm not sure she can. Unfortunately for her, I'm too selfish of a prick to care—until I do.

DEDICATION

To all the women who love the fun loving bad boys with soft hearts

1

Typical ghost town.

Monday nights at my bar, Happy Daze Tavern, always are. With summer about to start and no Monday night football, it's empty of all the townies who'd normally be hanging around. And though it's not good for my business, the tourists will be inundating my small town, Climax Cove, again next year so I'll enjoy it while I can. I love the silence.

If you knew me at all, that statement would confuse you.

I'm the fun guy, the one who has a smart-ass comment for every situation thrown my way. There's not much I take seriously—the polar opposite of my buddies, Marcus and Garrett. Isn't that the beauty of friendships though, you each bring something different to the plate?

"You want another?" I ask the cute brunette drowning her sorrows in my special for tonight—watermelon martini.

She's had three so far. The last one I made weaker than the drinks I make for the twenty-one-year-olds who come in here to celebrate their birthdays.

Hey, I was the loser who passed out on his birthday after

two hours of drinking and if I can help it, I'll save someone else from waking up with a black dick drawn on their face. I consider it my civic duty.

She shakes her head, her gaze fixed to the bottom of her glass.

"Wanna talk about it?" I ask, drying the few glasses that were used tonight.

She raises her head to look at me and I can see the fear in her hazel eyes when they meet mine across the mahogany lacquered bar top.

"Oh, you're the dive into my problems and fix them type of bartender?" She chuckles to herself, swirling the red liquid in her cup.

"Hey, sweetheart, I have enough to do, you just seemed like you needed to get something off your chest."

And don't think I haven't noticed what a nice chest it is.

I shrug and swivel around to the row of bottles lined up like soldiers behind the bar, starting to take stock of what I have left.

"Well, since you so kindly asked, my mom is getting married to a class A douchebag and has decided to sell my childhood home and move to Norway. What a woman from Kansas has in common with someone like *him*, I have no clue." She raises her glass to her plump lips and downs the rest of her drink.

"You're upset because your mom has decided to live her life? What were you expecting? To come home in five years and have your mom make you tomato soup and grilled cheese? Maybe play with your Barbies and look at your ribbons from the third-grade spelling bee?"

I lean back on the bar and cross my arms, watching her jaw drop lower and lower and lower until her plump lips form the perfect 'O'.

I'm trying really hard not to picture what she'd look like with my dick in it. I swear I am.

"Seriously? That's you consoling your customer?"

My tongue smacks off the roof of my mouth. "See that's where people have it all wrong. Bartenders aren't for warm hugs and pats on the back, they're for making you see reality. Yours is that your mom has raised you and now it's her time to live a little."

"What the hell does a guy like you know about it?"

Her eyes roam up and down my body. My worn-in jeans and ratty Happy Daze Tavern t-shirt probably don't make me appear like an upstanding single dad. She likely just sees an incredibly fit, attractive guy in his prime and though she won't admit it, she's seconds away from drool dribbling out of the corner of her mouth.

What? I'm just being honest.

I push off the bar and rest my crossed arms on the bar top right in front of her. "Let's just say, I know plenty. You look like you were well taken care of, so, I'd say your mom did her job. It's time for baby bird to leave the nest."

Her narrowed eyes stare into mine, testing me to see if I'll break. Little does she know that I was the champ of the fourth-grade staring contest. Poor Jenny Geiser became cross-eyed because of her super competitive nature and trying to beat me out on the playground.

"You might have a point, but you could say it nicer."

She blinks and I back away from her personal space, secretly scoring another point in the win column in my mind. Juvenile, I know.

"Why? It's the same end result." I shrug.

"Because being nice to someone—"

"When was I not nice? I spoke the truth, that's all." I nod to her glass. "Another?"

Her gaze moves to the clock. "No, I shouldn't."

"Okay." My hand moves to take her glass but she slides it away.

"You probably have some hot date later?" she asks.

Now, I want you to take note of what just happened. She thought I was an asshole two minutes ago when I was giving her some tough love. Now, she's either looking for lust or love.

"No date." I keep my reply short.

"Your girlfriend waiting for you?"

Girls have no idea how easy they are to figure out. If she just asked me if I wanted to go back to her apartment and fuck, I'd say yes. We don't need to waste time on the mental gymnastics.

"No girlfriend, and before you ask, no wife."

She sits there silent, watching as I dry a glass for a moment. "Well, thank you for the advice." She lays down a twenty on the bar top and stands to leave.

"You from around here?" I ask, not really wanting this sweet, young thing to leave.

"No. I mean, it's complicated. I've been here before but I just returned for the summer."

I set the now dry glass back in its spot under the bar. "You probably shouldn't be driving home."

She waves me off. "Yeah, I know. Don't worry I'm not going to."

I pick her twenty up off the bar. "You want me to call ol' Mo to drive you home? He's the town's unofficial taxi. Fair warning though his cataracts are getting pretty bad and he's half deaf."

She scrunches her eyebrows at me. "That's okay. Thanks for your...advice."

I put her money in the till and when I turn back she's

already at the door of the bar. "Sure thing. Have a good one." I wave my hand and hear the door shut behind her.

Fifteen minutes later, I'm closing up the bar when I spot the same girl staring into the window of Bread Box Bakery. Her long hair is twisted up in one of those messy buns all the girls seem to wear now, exposing her neck.

I will not think about what it would be like to run my tongue along the skin there.

I will not think about what it would be like to run my tongue along the skin there.

Damn, I just thought about it.

Oh well, sue me.

"Do you not have a home?" I call across the desolate street.

She startles and swivels around, finding me already crossing the street.

"Yes, I have an apartment. I was just looking."

"Have you been?"

She crinkles her eyebrows obviously not understand my question.

"Norma makes the best pies. My favorite is the chocolate. Those little chocolate shavings." I close my eyes and rub my tummy, as though I just popped one in my mouth. "Delicious."

She clears her throat. "No. I've never had them."

"Well, make that a pit stop this summer because..." I lean in close and lower my voice. "Rumor is she's closing shop at the end of the season."

For the first time tonight, the gold flecks in her eyes sparkle. "Really?"

"Why would I lie?"

She turns her body back to the window case, her hand plants on the glass.

"Listen." I look around seeing no one in sight, which isn't unusual at eleven o'clock on a Monday night. "I'm fairly sure that the last crime that happened in Climax Cove was when Ross McGee sold a library book at his garage sale, but I have this manly obligation to make sure you get home safe."

She grants me her attention, narrows her eyes and crosses her arms over her chest. She's cute with her jeans and Chucks, though her t-shirt could cling a little more if you ask me, but she's got curves and a stellar ass as I just happened to notice when I approached from across the street.

Oh, give me a break, I'm a male, aren't I?

She cocks a hip and puts her hand on her waist. "What makes you think I'd let some bartender walk me home and find out where I live?"

I hold my hands up in the air. "Okay, then you can come to my house." I grin.

"What about *all* your responsibilities?"

Ladies and gentlemen of the jury, please take note that she doesn't immediately tell me to piss off. She could've shot me down by now, but she hasn't.

"Lucky for you, I'm done for the night."

I don't go into specifics that my son, Toby, is at a sleep-over. Rule number one in the Single Dads Club is you don't tell a girl you're a dad right away. Especially if you're just looking for a one and done.

"Lucky for me? Maybe lucky for you." She arches one of her dark eyebrows.

I step closer, my hand landing on the glass beside her head. "Either way, you haven't declined my offer. I could make those troubles go away."

Her eyes meet mine and I do my best to let her see that

I'll light up her world one orgasm at a time. She shifts her stance. Her tomboy vibe doesn't scream that she's a one-night stand kinda of girl, but I can tell she wants me nonetheless.

"Don't sugar talk me like I'm some bimbo without a brain. I know the score if I go home with you. Right now, I'm just trying to figure out if you're worth it."

I pull my phone out of my pocket. "Should I call some references for you?"

She rolls her eyes. "Spare me."

Weaving out from under my arm, she walks straight toward my car.

"How did you know the Mustang was mine?" I ask.

She walks backward now in order to face me. "I didn't need to score a thirty-five on my ACT to know you're the type of guy who buys a sports car in this town."

A smile overtakes my entire face. I like this girl. She's a little spitfire and it seems like she can go toe-to-toe with me. Not many can.

She's quiet the entire ride and except for a text I notice she sends someone, she stares out the window as we wind through downtown to my house on the beach. It's not much, but it's made a home for Toby and myself for the past five years.

I park in my driveway, and she climbs out of the car. Usually, I don't take girls back to my place, but I can see she wasn't about to ask me to hers and after the shit I dealt with today down at the county office with permits and crap, I need to bury myself in someone tonight.

Yeah, yeah, don't be all holier than now. I didn't tie her up and kidnap her. She came willingly.

Click.

I blink at the light and when the round circles disappear I see that she's fiddling with her phone.

She smiles, tucks it into her back pocket and strolls up to my front door.

Woman on a mission. I like it.

"Sorry, that was a precaution. If you're thinking of doing anything to me, my friends will hunt you down and take pliers to your penis now that there's evidence on my phone. Even though," her eyes roam up and down my body again, "I can probably take you."

I squeeze by her on the front porch, inserting my key into the lock. Take that last part for the euphemism it was.

"Take me? Have you not noticed I'm about a foot taller than you and weigh probably sixty pounds more?" I cock my eyebrow and open the door.

She slides under my arm and walks right into my house before I've even opened the door all the way.

"For someone who thinks I might murder them, you sure are in a hurry," I say.

The door closes behind us, and I take a quick glance around ensuring there's no sign of Toby or his existence. Thankfully I forced him to clean up his stuff this morning so there's really no sign of him living here like when he was little.

"What can I say, I'm eager for some fun." She toes out of her Chucks and wiggles her toes at the same time she strips off her shirt.

Well, damn, I don't have to worry about her finding out about Toby, this girl is ready for the bedroom already.

I push my own shoes off, reaching down to take off my socks and when I strip off my t-shirt, her eyes zero in on my number one asset—the groin cleavage.

"You're a fan of the cleavage?" I smirk at her.

She scrunches her eyes, trying to figure out what I'm talking about.

"The V shape of my torso. Groin Cleavage?" I point to the deep indents of muscle near my hips that lead down to the big prize. "It may be one of my best features, but I promise, that's not all I offer."

I stalk toward her, unbuttoning my pants and letting them pool at my feet, stepping out of them never breaking my stride.

Practice, ladies, practice.

She walks backward, clearly taken back by my aggressive behavior and it's guaranteed, she doesn't do this very often. It's my job to show her how great sex without strings can be.

2

DANE

My fingers move to the button of her jeans as my lips descend on hers. A small moan escapes, causing my balls to clench and I press against her, just enough so that she's pinned to the wall behind her.

With one push, her jeans fall to the floor and I pull away from our kiss to look her over.

Damn, I am one lucky mofo.

She's in a pink matching panty and bra set that fits like a glove to every one of her curves. My dick rises to full salute and I'm at war with myself because though I definitely want to see her naked, I'm hesitant to take them off her because she's rocking this look.

"Damn, you're hot," I mumble.

She places her two hands on either side of my head and pulls me into a hard kiss. I can't remember the last time I had a demanding girl who knew what she wanted and wasn't afraid to use and abuse me. Here's hoping she scratches and bites, too.

Climbing me like a tree, her legs wrap around my waist, and my hands slide under the panties covering her ass.

When I squeeze her flesh in my hands, it draws another moan from her throat.

"Bedroom?" she whispers in my ear and then her teeth nibble on my lobe and pull.

"I like the way you think."

Her tits are pressed against my chest, the hardness of her nipples poking through her bra, teasing me with what I hope will be in my mouth in less than two minutes.

We reach the bedroom, and I toss her on the bed, strip down my boxer briefs, and climb toward her.

She spreads her legs and I nestle between them, letting my dick tease her center.

Her fingers flex over my shoulders, and I pull down one of her bra cups, sucking her nipple into my mouth.

"Oh," she pants. "More."

I scrape my teeth along her nipple before drawing it into my mouth again, then release it with a loud pop.

"Tell me, how do you want me to play with your tits? Do you want me to squeeze them, bite them, tweak your nipples between my fingers...fuck them?" I rub my thumb along her nipple, my chin resting on her chest, staring up at her.

"What you're doing is fine," she says a little breathlessly.

"Fine isn't a word in my vocabulary, babe. Earth shattering is though." I raise both eyebrows in question.

She shifts under me, looking a little confused and I realize that this girl has no idea what turns her on. I grin at her, happy to be the one to teach her.

"Want me to find all the spots that make you wet and boneless with pleasure?" I ask.

A smile turns up her lips and my dick twitches wanting the attention, the attention of said beautiful mouth.

"Sure."

I reach under her and undo her bra, sliding the straps down her shoulders to leave her bare for me.

"You have perfect tits. I'm gonna enjoy playing with them using my tongue and teeth."

Another sigh out of her.

Palming her left tit, my mouth devours her right, making good on the promise of my words. By the time I move to her other one, she's squirming and wiggling under me. Her legs lock around my waist, and she grinds against me, looking for any type of friction to give her some relief.

After one last bite to her nipple, I look up at her. "You want me?" I ask.

She nods enthusiastically. My kinda girl.

Enthusiasm goes a long way in the bedroom, ladies.

"Do you want my cock inside of you? Stroking you so deep that you're clenching around me while you come?"

"Mmm…" She moans and bites her plump bottom lip.

I inch farther down, casting a row of kisses down her flat stomach. When I reach the apex of her thighs, her hands bunch the sheets in her fists.

"Tonight, this pussy is mine, and I plan to feast until I get my fill."

Her eyes widen at my crude words, but she doesn't try to move me away.

Pushing her thighs up, I situate myself between her legs. I inhale deeply and lock gazes with her over her mound. "You smell like heaven."

Her face flushes red and her back arches. Damn, she looks so sexy lying under me, allowing me to pleasure her and do as I see fit.

First, I suck the satin fabric of her panties into my mouth using my tongue to moisten them thoroughly and let her feel just enough to push her to the good side of crazy. Eventually I pull the fabric aside and swipe my tongue along her slit.

"Oh..." She tilts her pelvis, silently begging me for more.

"Perfection." She smells and tastes a little sweet and musky at the same time, like the black currant martini I made in honor of the Fourth of July last year. I'm never going to be able to make another one of those drinks without sportin' wood again.

Another red blush fills her cheeks. Damn, a man could get used to that sheepish innocent type seduction. Any man other than me.

Rip.

I rip each side of her panties, and a low groan escapes her.

"I need all of you and these," I hang the fabric off my finger, flinging them across the room, "would have taken too long to get off."

Without any further discussion, my head finds its new home between her legs, licking and sucking every drop she'll give me. She tries to close her thighs when I twirl my tongue around her clit, but my hands are too fast, pressing them to the mattress below her.

"Oh my God. You're so good."

I peek from one eye to see her head fallen on the mattress and her right hand now fondling her tit. I contemplate bringing her all the way to orgasm, teasing her until I plunge into the depths of her pussy just to feel the clench around me.

I have a feeling this girl has never had sex where you masturbate to the memory for days and since I'm a giver and everything, I'm going to deliver.

Relieving her thigh from my hand, I thrust two fingers

into her warmth and she bucks so hard, I'm afraid her pelvic bone will knock my teeth in.

"I knew you'd be good, but seriously, what have you taken, sex mastery classes from some guru or something?"

My mouth leaves her now wet and dripping pussy to find her eyes zeroed in on me. "If you can form a coherent sentence, I'm not doing my job."

I push the threshold of her depths arching until a low inaudible sound ruptures from her throat. There you go. That's it, baby, give it to me.

My tongue twirls making her clit my own plaything until she bucks again, her thighs tense, her back arches and she grips the sheet so tight in her fists her knuckles turn white. I don't relent the pace of my fingers or my tongue until her defeated body falls to the mattress and her fingers weave through the strands of my hair.

Checking up on her, I rub my chin along her stomach until we're face to face.

"Would you like to find out how delicious you taste?"

I don't wait for her to answer. Instead, I bend down and kiss the rest of her breath from her lungs. Her fingers continue to fiddle with the strands of hair on my neck as my dick now gets teased with how wet and waiting she is for it.

She moans when I break the kiss and reach across the bed to my dresser. Her hands explore my body while I dig to find the condoms I hide so Toby never finds them. Finally, with my dick begging for relief, a foil packet miraculously is in my grasp.

"Feel honored, I haven't worked that hard for a condom in ages."

She giggles, the first sign out of her that she's the innocent girl I pegged her for back at the bar.

The giggle fades quickly and she rolls me on my back, taking the condom wrapper from my grip.

"Allow me." She smirks.

I clasp my hands behind my head. "I like this."

"Well," She rips the foil open. "I do like to repay favors."

No way this girl has had a lot of one-night stands, but she knows how to put on a condom, which means I'm not her first bull. Thank fucking God.

"I'm sure we could work out a payment schedule."

She giggles again. This heart spurring, warming laugh that does something to my stomach.

Then she straddles me, guiding my dick inside her and this time *my* head is the one that falls back into my pillows.

"Shit, you're as tight as a fist."

Those gold flecks in her eyes sparkle again and her hands land on my chest as she rides me like a professional cowgirl. Give the girl the bull-riding prize.

"And these tits are so fuckable, I can't keep my hands to myself." I cup each one, massaging them in my palms. Nothing like a good set of C's.

When I buck up, she cries out. "You feel amazing," she says, arching her back and letting her hands land on my thighs.

"Your pussy is meant for my dick. Perfect. Fucking. Fit." I punctuate the last three words as I thrust up into her.

She eyes me below her, a redness in her cheeks that could be from the compliments or the fact she's expending all her energy on top of me. Her hips rotate faster, her hands gripping my thighs.

Reluctantly, I move my hands to her hips to keep the rhythm we've established and my gaze zeros in on her tits as they sway and bounce with every movement.

We grind, our fucking fast and desperate. I can't get

enough of her, and I find myself inventorying the many types of booze behind my bar in order to slow myself down and let this moment last longer. She's soft under my hands but her touch is firm and tense as though she's thinking what I am—how the hell can we prolong this?

Needing to get as deep as I can, I flip her over onto her back. She rolls over one more time and doesn't delay getting onto her hands and knees.

That's what I'm talking about.

"Perfect tits and a perfect ass. How'd I get so lucky?"

My fingers mold to her hips and I thrust my straining cock into her fast and fierce. I draw myself out and slam back in. We both groan. Needing to be closer to her, I slow my movements, my chest resting on top of her back while I plant open mouth kisses along her skin. She arches her head back giving me access to her neck. But it's not enough, I crave her kiss, so, I reach across and turn her chin toward me so I can ravish her mouth while my cock grinds in and out of her.

The spark between us ignites into an inferno. We both part from the kiss. My pace increases and her hands fist the sheets while her forehead rests on the bed.

"You ready to come all over my cock?" *I sure as fuck am ready for her to.*

"Yes." Her voice is breathless and the tone I expect from a woman when I'm fucking her.

"I'm gonna come, but I'm a gentleman." I smack her ass. "Ladies first."

The minute my palm makes contact with her ass cheek, her pussy clenches around me, her back arches, her arms straighten.

I pump one more time then still inside of her, half wishing I wasn't wearing a condom so that I could feel her scorching heat on my own skin. I'll be imagining tonight while I'm stroking my stick for at least a week. If she stays and I can have her again tonight, it'll be two weeks worth of material for my beat off wheel footage.

Her trembling body falls to the mattress, and I slide to the side of her, catching my own breath.

She looks over at me with brown strands of hair sticking to her sweat covered forehead. "I'm a little scared to ask how many partners you've had since you're that good."

I slide down the bed. "Stick around and I'll show you a few more tricks." I wink and walk into my bathroom, dispose of the condom in the trash and head back into the bedroom.

She's already positioning her bra back over her perfect rack.

"I should get going. How far away are we from town?"

I lean my back along the headboard. "Stay awhile." I slide the strap of her bra back down her arm.

"Isn't the point of a one-night stand that you leave after?" She lets a nervous chuckle escape.

I eliminate the distance between us, my lips hovering over hers. "The point of a one-night stand is to fuck *all* night long and then you leave in the morning and we never see each other again. I think I have at least three more orgasms in me. You?" I smirk and her lips turn up in a smile. "Is that a yes?" I pepper open-mouthed kisses along her collarbone while my hand slides the other side of her bra down.

"You do make a convincing argument." Her hands slide around to the back of my head, locking me in place.

I'm true to my word, proving my argument three more times while we fall asleep, wake up and bang throughout the night.

When I wake up in the morning, she's gone, and so is my Mustang with a note.

To the great and powerful O guru,

Last night was fun. Had to get to work. I'll park your car outside the bar for you and tuck the keys under the mat.

Yours screaming,
    So Satisfied

What kind of one-night stand takes your car the next morning? It's called the walk of shame, not grand theft auto.

3

DANE

Three Months Later...

"Dad, it wasn't my fault, I was just joking around with her!" Toby's excuse rushes out as soon as he walks through Happy Daze doors.

I know, kids shouldn't be in bars, but Happy Daze Tavern is now Happy Daze Tavern and Grill, so technically this is a restaurant too.

"First day of school and the principal calls me?" I continue handing out the drinks to the Single Dads Club crew for the meeting tonight. None of them will judge me on the fact that my kid decided to act like he was going to kiss a girl in his class.

What can I say? The apple didn't fall far.

"She was all drama. I mean, I wasn't actually going to kiss her. I don't even like her." He sits on a stool and plops his backpack on the bar.

I grab him a juice box from the fridge and place it in front of him.

"Just stay away from her."

He pulls out a stack of papers, and I sign the letter sent out to say we've discussed the problem.

"She's dumb."

We exchange worksheets and notebooks until I've seen all the assignments he's brought home and provided all the required signatures. Seriously, schools these days do not trust kids. I have to mark off whether he read, initial his planner and acknowledge what grades he got on any and all tests. You'd think I was Michael Jordan based on the number of autographs I scribble every day.

"That's not going to help your case. Just play with Cooper and the boys."

His eyes roll to the back of his head and then his forehead thuds to the bar. Who knew eight-year-old boys had such a flare for the dramatic. I didn't even punish him.

"Cooper is the one who started the whole thing! He dared me to kiss her."

I hold my hand up in the air. "What? You just said you were never going to kiss her."

He lets out an exasperated breath as though I'm the annoying one in this exchange.

"I wasn't! Jeez, you just don't understand."

"Parents never do," Charlie adds as she slides behind me to work her shift. After securing her apron, she leans over and rustles his mop of brown hair. "In ten years, you can escape him," she whispers loud enough for me to hear.

"Nice," I comment, and she shrugs, bouncing on the balls of her feet down to the other side of the bar. Of course, she's in a good mood, Garrett's sitting over by the dartboard and she has an unrestricted view.

"Hey, I'm always on your side. Remember that." Now it's my hands rustling his hair, but he quickly slides back so I can no longer reach him. I swear I was all about Legos and riding my bike at eight. I don't remember all these hormonal mood swings.

"After I do my homework, can I go over to the new bakery?"

My gaze goes to the window and to the bakery across the street. They opened their doors today and it hasn't escaped me that there's been a constant flow of customers in and out. I hadn't been by yet, but Marcus brought over some cookies from there and they tasted okay.

"Yeah. Sure. I have the meeting and then we'll be heading home anyway."

He nods, knowing the drill. I wish Toby had a normal childhood and not a dad who owns a bar, but I grew up as a bar owner's son and look at me—I turned out more than okay. The difference is, I had a mom who helped to raise me. But the last thing Toby needs in his life is his mother.

Leaving Toby to do his work, I walk toward Charlie who is currently pretending to be wiping down the counter. The only problem is that her chin rests on her hand and she's mindlessly buffing the same circular pattern into the bar top below her rag while her gaze fixates on Garrett. Not that he notices.

"Why don't you just ask him out?"

She startles, straightening her back and tossing the rag under the counter.

"What? Who?"

I raise my eyebrow, crossing my arms over my chest. "Let's not play dumb," I say.

"What's up with Toby? What happened at school today?"

I wave her concern off. "Just messing around with some girl. Nothing huge, but nothing like having to speak to Principal Bundy on the first day of school. I'm sure she loved that."

"Well, you do still hold a reputation at Climax Cove Elementary." She laughs.

"They should make a plaque." I position my hands in the air. "Dane Murray, Most Detentions."

"Not exactly something they want to broadcast." Her eyes veer through the front windows of the bar. "Did you see the new bakery?"

"Clever name, Mad Batter," I remark.

"I know, right? She loves Alice in Wonderland."

"You know the woman who bought it from Norma?" I ask.

A couple months ago, Charlie brought in cupcakes that literally melted in my mouth. Then all of a sudden, she stopped and when I asked her about it, she said she'd ask for more. She never did bring any more in and as time went on, I must've forgotten about them. My mouth waters at the memory.

"It's my friend. The cupcake girl." A smirk crosses her lips.

"Really? Shit, I've wasted a whole day."

I walk away, rounding the bar top. "Let's go get a cupcake and then you can finish your math."

Toby jumps off, the pencil rolling off the bar and onto the floor. I don't have to repeat myself. Toby and sweets are like peanut butter and jelly. Never one without the other.

"Dad, I'm old enough." He shrugs his hand out of mine as we're crossing the street.

When did eight become thirteen?

Placing my hand on his elbow, I guide him through the cars driving through downtown.

Pink, blue and green balloons are on either side of the bakery and a sign that says, 'Now Open' hangs above the door. Inside, cute white tables are filled with moms and their daughters eating cupcakes and drinking tea or coffee.

Not in the mood to chitchat, I walk to the case where there are still a few rows of cupcakes in different flavors lining the glass case.

"Toby, do you want a sample?"

We both look down at the small voice, finding my buddy's daughter, Lily, holding a tray full of little frosted cakes.

"You got a job?" Toby asks Lily and she smiles.

"I'm helping. Cat said she'd buy me the new Barbie if I did a good job."

Toby laughs and grabs a sample.

"You look adorable," I say to Lily who is dressed up as Alice in Wonderland. Her blonde hair a perfect match to the real thing.

"Thanks."

Then she's gone, and I'm trying to see over the crowd of customers who Charlie's friend is. First Charlie, and now Lily. I have my suspicions, but I could be wrong. It does happen on occasion.

Finally, a lifetime later, Toby and I are at the counter and Cat stands there with her blonde hair pinned back and an apron that says, 'We are all Mad Here.'

"Cat?" I ask, peeking my head around her, trying to see through the four by six cut-out window into the kitchen area in the back.

"Dane!" She says my name loud enough for everyone in

the restaurant to hear and a clatter of something dropping in the kitchen rings out into the front part of the bakery.

"Miss Cat. Is this your bakery?" Toby asks beside me, and she shifts her gaze to him.

"Hi, Toby!" Again with the loud talking.

I know before I even see her who it is. I may not have known her name the night I took her home, but I sure as shit know it now because she's been on my jock ever since she found out I was the single dad of Toby Murray, a camper assigned to her over the summer.

"No, I don't own it, but you know who does," Cat says in a sugary sweet voice.

"I do?" he asks, clearly confused about what's going on.

"Mad Baker," she calls over her shoulder. "There are a couple people here to see you."

A second later, a pink-cheeked Ava Pearson walks out from around the corner with a red and black checkered apron wrapped around her stamped with 'Do you want to pet my white rabbit?'

Is she fucking kidding me? There's kids around and she has on an apron inviting any Tom, Dick and Harry to pet her rabbit?

"Miss Ava!" Toby pushes me into the counter to get to her.

She opens her arms and wraps them around his body into a tight hug. Since summer camp, they've had a bond. He might have been a hellion, but after I distanced myself from her and stopped trying to get her back into my bed, it got better for Toby. His needs come before I do. See what I did there?

"You bake all this?" he asks, and she nods, her gaze finding mine across the room.

"Congratulations," I say, trying to act as though I don't

want to smash my fist into the glass case like The Incredible Hulk and crumble them all in my mouth like Cookie Monster.

"Thank you." She looks to Cat, whose eyes are bouncing between us with a fucking smirk on her lips. She's so wrong with her assumption, but then again, she probably doesn't even know that I've had Ava already. A few hundred times if you count all the showers I've beat off to using my memories of her.

"Cat, give them anything they want." Her gaze flicks to mine for a microsecond. "On the house."

"What's 'on the house' mean?" Toby asks, as Ava tucks the longer strands of his hair behind his ear.

"Free. You pick whatever you want and it's free." She smiles down at him and his eyes light up.

"Thanks, Miss Ava!"

He runs over to the case, and Cat opens up a box ready for his order.

"So, you're the one."

"Excuse me?" She walks over to her display shelf, straightening some teacups.

"Charlie used to bring your cupcakes into the bar. They're amazing."

She nods, her attention staying on the ceramic teapots for sale. "Good to know you enjoyed them. I love seeing people's expressions when they're eating my goodies." She turns around, shoving her hands in the pockets of her apron.

I avoid the obvious joke she's led me into since I'm not sure she'd appreciate it. Still, there's about a million different ways our re-acquaintance could play out here.

"You cut me off." I don't ask because it's clear she did.

She nods once to confirm my suspicions. After our two

times together, and stealing my car, we've had a love-hate relationship that teetered more on the hate side. Especially after I found out her dad was the camp owner, Vic Pearson, my half-Brazilian buddy I know could sure hurt me if he wanted to.

"You act like I'm a dealer."

"Those cupcakes might as well have been crack."

I won't tell her, but I went through withdrawal, sampling cupcakes at every store only to find nothing comparable. I even ordered them online and had them delivered. Nothing was the same as those gooey, moist cupcakes Charlie had brought in. Which now I find out were made by my secret fling, if you can even call it that.

She smiles, obviously flattered by my cupcake crack addiction.

"So, why'd you do it?"

She shrugs. "I really need to get back to work." She turns, but I take her elbow and swing her back around.

"I thought those nights together were mutual?" I whisper, so we won't be the town gossip. Marcus and Cat's affair is down to embers now and the gossip queens of Climax Cove are looking for new material to fill their text boxes.

"They were. Don't worry, you didn't break my heart or anything." She shrugs.

I stare at her, and those gold flecks that seem to spark with any type of strong emotion she's feeling are void.

"Well, good. I like to make it clear that nothing more will happen." I shift my weight on my feet.

She smiles, one that doesn't reach her eyes. "You were crystal clear, Dane. Especially when you blamed me for not telling you that I was Vic's daughter. If I recall, you weren't too worried about my name that first night." She disappears into the kitchen, and a feeling of guilt and shame slips into me from my subconscious. The argument a few weeks into camp after I found out she was Toby's camp counselor floating back to my conscious. Yeah, I was a dick, but she wasn't exactly a sweetheart like the real Alice in Wonderland either.

"Here you go," Cat hands me a box. "I did an assortment, but make sure you try the Neapolitan one. I think you'll like it."

I take the box from her hands, my gaze still on the kitchen where clanking and pounding echoes out of.

"Do me a favor?" My eyes flick to hers, and she straightens her back. "Tell the Mad Batter I'd like to order two dozen chocolate cupcakes with whipped cream frosting and chocolate shavings."

"Oh, I'm not sure she's doing special orders," Cat insists, already shaking her head.

"I'll be here tomorrow to pick them up."

"Dane..."

I turn around and spot Toby chomping down on a chocolate and white cookie near the door. "I'll pay double for the inconvenience."

Not bothering to see Cat's reaction, I tap Lily on the head on our way out.

"Keep pushing."

She smiles, and the door chime sounds as we push open the glass doors.

4

The door chime rings and I send a small prayer up that it was Dane leaving.

I glimpse out the cut-out into the storefront and catch him and Toby crossing the street.

"What's going on with you two?" Cat asks, popping up in front of me and blocking my line of vision.

"Nothing." I circle back around to hide in the kitchen.

I asked for Cat's help because come on, she's like sugar on a stick. Sweet and sophisticated, she could talk anyone into buying my goodies. Baked goods, get your mind out of the gutter.

The door between the kitchen and the storefront swings open and Cat pushes through to join me. "I think you're lying. You're always so angry around him. Why?" She saddles up on a stool in front of the frosting station.

"He's a condescending asshole who always gets what he wants."

She nods. "That about sums up Dane Murray, but why do you care?"

She's fishing, and I don't blame her especially since she's

all in love and stuff with his best friend Marcus now. The fact we'll be thrown together is inevitable. She probably doesn't want it awkward for everyone.

"The way he acted during camp this summer. I mean he propositions me at the lake with the other campers there, including his son. Constantly undermined my authority with the kids, coming in and stealing the show when he picked Toby up. I mean, I feel bad for Toby having a father who feels the need to be the center of attention all the time." I pick up the pink icing bag to finish the cotton candy cupcakes I had a special order for.

"Okkkaaayyy," Cat purposely draws out the word, and I know she doesn't get it because she doesn't know the crux of the situation. I slept with him and I felt weird about it since the second I woke up the next morning.

"Obviously not weird enough not to go back for seconds.

My subconscious sneers at me. Whatever.

It was my first one-night stand. I'm not upset that I did it. Dane Murray is clearly an expert on pleasing a woman which is the only reason I went back for round two.

It was the week after when he made me *really* regret my decision.

I HAD WORKED THAT ENTIRE WEEK ON MY CABIN TO MAKE IT FUN and educational. I needed to prove to not only my dad but also my peers, that I could do this. My dad, Vic, owns the camp and started it years ago for children of single parents to spend the summer doing fun activities so their parents could work. Then one weekend out of the month the parents are welcome to spend the night with their camper and fish, swim or hike in the mountains.

Since it was my first year, I got a day group, the eight-year-

olds. Thankful I wouldn't be spending the night in the cabins and could have my own apartment. I was excited for what the summer would bring. Then my mom lobbed the grenade, telling me that after the summer, I'd have no home to return to. That it was time I grew up and decided what I wanted to do with my life. She was marrying her boyfriend—whom I hated—and moving to the other side of the world.

Which landed me on the stool of Happy Daze Tavern with Dane serving me drinks. He thinks he got one over on me, making my last couple drinks virgins, but I knew. That was one of the only reasons I went home with him—because instead of plying me with drinks to make me an easy lay, he did the opposite.

That night could very well be the best sex I'll ever have in my life. Not that I'll ever boost his ego even more by confessing that.

A couple of weeks later there was Dane, dropping his son off to my cabin for his day at camp. Something fueled inside me and I'm not even sure what. The fact he took me home when he had a son? When I replay the conversation, I do recall him implying he had something big he was responsible for, but he wasn't specific.

I greeted Toby, told him to join the other campers and then politely asked to speak to Dane alone outside the cabin.

"Do you steal the car of everyone you bang or should I feel special?" He had his cocky grin splashed across his face, and his hands tucked into the pockets of his black track pants.

I swallowed hard when I thought of the groin cleavage hidden under the white t-shirt. The memory of my fingers exploring the curves and crevices of that perfect V were front and center in my mind.

"I borrowed it and I did it so I wouldn't disturb you."

He chuckled, rolling back on his flip-flops. "I appreciate it, but next time call Al's Taxi."

I might have been new to town, but everyone knew Al only

does pick-ups and drop-offs between seven and seven. Most of his clientele are residents of Forest Hill Retirement Home.

"There won't be a next time."

That grin grew wider and cockier. My hand itched to slap him. His eyes flowed up and down my body, igniting my skin like an uncontrolled wildfire.

"I have to say this whole you being Toby's counselor puts a damper on it, sure, but I think we could hide it. Though, from what I remember you're quite the screamer." *He licked his lips.*

My hands clenched at my sides for a second. "Not going to happen." *I placed my hands on my hips.*

"Hey, sweetheart. Dane." *My dad walked by the cabin with his group of teenage survivalists.*

"Hey."

"So, that's it then." *The grin left his lips and he huffed a sarcastic laugh.*

"What?" *I ask.*

"You're already taken." *He raised his hands up in the air.* "Listen, I don't take another guy's chick and sure as shit don't take Vic's."

He started backing up and I should have left well enough alone. Let him believe what he wanted, but I spoke up, which twisted things more.

"He's my dad, asshole."

His eyes widened, and he stumbled to the side as though I just shot him with a tranquilizer. "You're Vic Pearson's daughter?

"Yes," *I answered, and he stepped back farther than he did when he thought I was my dad's girlfriend.*

He looked at me long and hard. "I see it now. The resemblance. Fuck me. Listen, I'll keep quiet if you do, but why the fuck didn't you tell me?"

"Excuse me, I don't recall you telling me you were a father." *I crossed my arms over my chest, and his eyes dipped to my breasts. I didn't change my stance because he could look, but he was never touching again.*

"Fuck, let's just make sure we keep our distance from now on, okay?" He was practically half way up the hill by then.

"Fine with me! You weren't that memorable anyway."

Why did I have to stir the pot?

He barreled back down the hill and leaned in really close to me.

"Don't undermine what we shared. You and I both know what happened in that room. We just need to keep it in the beat off reel now, got it?"

A shiver ran up my spine with him so close to me.

"Got it."

He nodded and then all but jogged away where I spied him meeting up with another dad at the top of the hill as they disappeared into the woods toward the parking lot.

Stupid me sought him out at the bar a few days later because I couldn't get him off my mind. What happened in his office is still burned into my memory as is my discovery the next day. Then we had our rip-roaring fight after Toby got in trouble at camp one day and that sealed the deal. Dane Murray could go to hell for all I cared.

"OH, I ALMOST FORGOT," CAT INTERRUPTS ME.

I place the final pink cupcake in the box.

"Dane wants two dozen cupcakes for tomorrow."

"I'm not taking special orders."

Cat's gaze flicks to the box I'm covering and taping.

"From him," I finish, and she places an order sheet down on the table in front of me.

I read the order. Chocolate with whipped cream and chocolate shavings. What the hell is he up to?

"Do you have his phone number?" I ask Cat, and her eyes widen.

"Um, let me see." She pulls her phone out, but we both know she has it. "Yeah." She scribbles it down on the order form and slides it back over to me.

I wipe my hands on my apron and pull my own phone out, texting.

ME: For a special order, I need a full day's notice and half the deposit.

The three dots appear instantly. Does this man have nothing better to do in his life?

Dane: Okay, I'll pick them up in two days. I'll send Toby over with the deposit. Unless you'd rather me hand deliver it? I'm good with my hands...as you know.

I tighten my grip on my phone and ignore his innuendo.

ME: Toby can drop off the deposit and pick up the cupcakes.

Dane: Toby's running it over right now, but sorry, you'll have to see my smiling face for pick-up.

Me: You need help.

Dane: Just need the cupcakes, but thanks for the advice. Want me to offer you some?

Me: I'm perfectly fine.

Dane: Ever consider anger management?

MY THUMBS PRESS HARD ON THE N AND O AND I ADD A zillion exclamation points.

DANE: SEE WHAT I MEAN? DON'T TAKE LIFE SO SERIOUSLY, Mad Batter.

Me: Wednesday afternoon you can pick up your cupcakes.

Dane: Looking forward to it. We could close for lunch and have some fun with frosting.

Me: You're seriously demented. I'm stopping this texting now.

Dane: Or we could sext! Let me visualize you in only the apron for a moment.

Dane: Okay, I'm ready now.

I CAN JUST IMAGINE HIM OVER AT HIS BAR, SMILING AWAY LIKE he's got one over on me. Not likely.

ME: I STRIPPED OFF MY APRON AND I'M STANDING IN THE kitchen wearing a chocolate peanut butter bikini made of frosting.

THERE, THAT SHOULD DO IT.

DANE: DAMN YOU DON'T PLAY FAIR. SOMEONE MUST'VE TOLD

you my favorite cupcake. It warms my heart that you remembered.

Me: Bye.

Dane: See you tonight...in my imagination while I'm fisting my dick.

MY STOMACH FLIPS AND I PLACE MY FREE HAND OVER IT TO reprimand myself for reacting to his dirty talk.

I toss my phone on the table and clench my fists.

"Fondant, I need fondant." Anything to beat and knead to get that man out of my head.

"You're so red," Cat comments. "You're flushed." The door chime rings and Cat peeks around the corner then turns and points at me. "One day, you're going to fess up."

She disappears out front and I collapse to the stool, inhaling a deep breath. Hours of kneading and stirring and frosting go by and the only thing on my mind is Dane.

Why am I finding myself attracted to him again? Because you opened a bakery across from his bar, dipshit. How did I think I could continue to dodge him? I knew I'd see him eventually, but I honestly didn't think he'd want anything to do with me. After all, he was the one who was so appalled that I was Vic's daughter.

Speak of the devil, my dad walks through the swinging door into the kitchen area.

"What a success, huh?" He takes a seat on the stool Cat just got up from. "You look hot, sweetheart. Maybe you could open the back door? I could install a screen so no bugs would get in." He stands up and makes his way to the back to check out the door.

"I'm okay, Dad. Thanks."

"You don't look okay." He swings the back door open. "I

was at the Single Dads Club get-together across the street and Dane brought a box of your cupcakes in, but he refused to share. That's a great sign, huh? I think you made the right choice by buying Norma out."

My dad, my forever cheerleader.

His silver hair shines under the florescent lights.

"Yeah, time will tell."

"Sweetheart, I don't think you need time, this place is going to make it. I feel it."

I cross my fingers and hold them up in the air. "I hope so."

He kisses my cheek. "Don't worry, you're living your dream. And the best part is we can see each other everyday now."

I nod. "Thanks, Dad." I pat his hand that's resting on my upper arm.

If only I believed in myself as much as my dad does.

5

DANE

"Why are you trying to start something up?" Marcus asks the next day during a lunch at Double D's Diner.

I chomp down on my double cheeseburger, trying to hide my smile. As I chew, it takes a lot more effort to hide my amusement at the fact that I'm pissing Ava off. I'm not even sure why I'm doing it. Something to do in this small-ass town maybe.

Once I swallow and wash it down with a sip of my Coke, I lean back in the booth. Garrett and Marcus both stare directly at me from the other side.

"I'm helping her out." I shrug. "Starting a business can be hard."

They share a *yeah-right* look but don't argue. All three of us own our own companies in Climax Cove and know how difficult those early days can be. Garrett had the biggest uphill climb but he also didn't have his dad breathing down his damn neck all the time like I do.

"She doesn't like you though," Marcus comments, dipping his fry into ketchup and popping it into his mouth.

"Why is that exactly?" Garrett chimes in.

Usually, I'm the first one to brag about getting laid, but with Ava, I kept it quiet because she's Vic's daughter and I do not want that to circle back to him. We're acquaintances more than friends, but I have a lot of respect for the guy and I'd hate for him to think less of me.

"Somehow she's immune to my charismatic personality." I pop my own fry into my mouth.

Dennis, the owner of the diner, must have finally changed the oil in the fryer. This grub is better than usual.

"I'd say half of Climax Cove is immune to your unique personality." Marcus sips his drink and studies me for a second. "Cat told me something interesting last night."

Garrett shifts his attention away from his BLT double bacon sandwich.

I roll my eyes. "Whatever it was, I'm sure she's wrong."

Marcus' eyes stay zeroed in on me while Garrett's gaze moves in my direction, questioning.

"She said Ava was so squirrely after you left, she kneaded ten batches of fondant. Cat thinks you two might actually like each other?" He raises his eyebrows, revealing the blue eyes so many women swoon over.

"Really?" Garrett leans back, crosses his arms around his chest like he'd rather hear me admit I like her than eat his sandwich. If you knew Garrett, you'd know how huge that is. The guy is like a big, beefy mountain man. He needs a lot of fuel to stay upright.

I crumple up my napkin and toss it on the table. "Please. Ava Pearson screams commitment, and I think you both know by now, there's only one person I'm committed to and he's about this high." I stick my arm out of the booth and raise it a little above my shoulder.

Again, they each share a look of *whatever*. "You do

understand you committed to your dad when you took over the bar," Marcus smiles and digs back into his plate.

"You also committed to this town by helping with the Fourth of July parade and the carnival at the end of every summer," Garrett says, then sips his iced tea, waiting for me to agree.

"That's different, and you both know it. I'm talking about anything beyond a hit and split."

Garrett shrugs and picks up his sandwich.

"Neither one of you can talk," I say.

Marcus tilts his head.

"Okay, you've committed to Cat now, but Garrett." He never even looks up from his sandwich because he knows what I'm going to say. "You don't commit."

"He also doesn't go on search and rescue missions for pussy either." Marcus pushes his plate forward having devoured his Reuben sandwich.

"Anything else boys?" Debbie picks up Marcus' plate.

"Thanks, Debbie," he says.

"Hey, did you guys change the oil in the fryer?" I ask. "The fries taste awesome today."

Debbie takes her free hand and slaps me on the back of the head. "I swear if I didn't still see the cute sandy-haired boy with pinchable cheeks, I'd kick you out of here." Bending over, she takes her forefinger and thumb grabbing my cheek and squeezing harder than I remember her doing when I was little.

She mumbles to herself as she walks toward the kitchen. I place my hand on my now sore cheek. Marcus and Garrett laugh sharing a look that says, 'what did I really expect to happen?'

I shrug and dig back into my meal. Charlie's covering the

bar, but I need to head back for my appointment with the vodka supplier.

"What are you going to do with two dozen cupcakes anyway?" Marcus asks after finishing his meal. Not that I have a clue how he's finished when all he's done during lunch is stick his nose into my business.

"I'm going to sell them to my customers as dessert."

Marcus' forehead crinkles. I swear if we did a line up in a police station for someone to pick who out of us is a dad, they'd pick Marcus for sure. He's got all the dad looks mastered like he's practiced in a mirror or some shit.

"She doesn't need to know. I'm experimenting with something. If it works, believe me, it'll only benefit her and her company." I wipe my mouth with my napkin, crumple it up and place it on my plate.

"You're playing with fire if she already doesn't like you." Garrett finishes his own meal, digging into his pocket for his wallet. He's on a deadline to get two cabins finished before winter hits so he can make bank by renting them out. The guy might just be a secret millionaire who buys stock in flannel shirts since that's all he ever seems to wear.

"Hey, for those of us like me," I point to myself, "tourist season is drawing to an end and she just opened up a business. Happy Daze makes the majority of its profit from April to October."

They each stare blankly at me. I'm sure they assumed that was the case, but it was a hard lesson I learned the first year I took over the business from my dad—a lesson that almost closed our doors.

"If I didn't know better, I'd say you're *very* committed to Climax Cove." Marcus laughs and Garrett soon joins in.

I shake my head, slide out of the booth and walk over to Debbie to pay my bill.

"Oh, don't be so sensitive, Dane," Marcus is behind me now as I pull out my money and focus my attention on Debbie.

"You know I was joking, Debbie. I wouldn't be your number one customer if I didn't love your food." I walk around the counter and hold my hands out for a hug. She tries to get away, but I wrap my arms around her shoulders and pull her snug against me.

"Salad for you next time." She's laughing, knowing the day I eat a salad is the day I can't bring a fork to my mouth. Not going to happen.

"I love you, Deb." I smack my lips on her head and make the exaggerated noise as I back away from her. "See you tomorrow."

I walk by Marcus and Garrett as I head for the door. "Jackasses." I nod to them and walk out of the diner and head straight to the bar. And I somehow manage to do all that without sneaking a look at the bakery.

LATER THAT NIGHT AFTER I'VE CLOSED UP HAPPY DAZE, I'M going through my mail on the bar when something catches my attention out of the corner of my eye. Investigating where it's coming from, I stand up and look across the street. It's pitch black in the bakery except for a flashlight in search of something.

I jump over my bar, swiping my keys from the counter on the way. Hustling out of the bar, I glance up and down the street. It's once again vacant of anyone, which proves my point to Marcus and Garrett. Tourist season is already drawing to a close as October approaches. I lock the door and peer over to the bakery. The flashlight is still there.

Clicking Ava's name on my phone, I hear the faintest ring of her cell, meaning she's in there somewhere. There's no turning back now even though I only have my fists to protect myself with. Hopefully, I can channel Bruce Lee or something.

The glass door to the bakery opens when I pull on the handle and I mentally pocket the advice to tell Ava to lock her doors when the business is closed. Climax Cove police officers earn their paychecks by directing traffic during the summer.

I slide in and search for any sign of the spunky brunette who's always on my case. She's nowhere to be found, so I tiptoe further back, noticing to my dismay the cupcake case is empty.

A thud echoes throughout the quiet space. "Fuck!" There's some more grumbling I can't make out and then, "Where the hell is it? Stupid, Ava, so stupid. Why did you ever think you could do this?"

I should let her know I'm here.

"Hello? Yes. This is Ava Pearson from Mad Batter." Another pause. "My power just went out. Yeah. I don't know where the fuse box is." The flashlight moves and shines right past me.

You're being a dick. Let her know you're here and help her, my inner self keeps repeating.

I click the green button on my phone again.

"Ugh. Hold on a second." The lighted phone pulls away from her face, she presses ignore. "Ugh, asshole." Then places it back to her cheek. "Sorry, where would I find the fuse box?"

"My guess is back in the storage room," I say.

She jumps so far back, she trips over something and falls, her phone sliding across the floor.

I bend down and pick it up.

"Ma'am? Ma'am?" Frank's never sounded so scared.

"Hey, Frank. It's Dane. No, I got it, no need for the fire department to come down. Yeah, I saw from across the street. We'll call back if we need you guys. Yeah, see you on Trivia night."

I click the red button and turn on the flashlight on her phone.

She's getting to her feet, brushing off her ass after tripping on a bag of flour.

"Here." I hold my hand out for her, but she refuses to take it.

"I'm fine. Knocking would be the polite thing to do." She blocks the light from the flashlight with her arm and I lower it a little.

"Well, I'm an asshole so you shouldn't expect much." I shrug, taking her phone with me into the storage room.

"You don't have to help me. I'm sure the fire department would be willing," she rambles as she follows me.

"They should be available for *actual* fires."

"I imagine fires are like crimes in this town—almost nonexistent."

I turn around, flashing the light toward my face so she can see me. "You'd be wrong then. Forest fires." I tap my head and all I hear is her huff.

"You think you're so smart."

She's embarrassed, I get it, so I don't rub in the fact I am fucking smart.

"Would you rather me not know how to fix your breaker?"

She hems and haws for a second. "I don't understand. I was in the middle of making a huge batch of frosting and then total darkness."

"Was that your way of asking me for help?" I open the box, purposely not touching any of the breakers.

"I didn't know I had to ask since you took it upon yourself to sneak into my shop, scare the crap out of me and then walk to the storage room."

"And I haven't even told you to keep your doors locked when you're closed yet. But most people say please and thank you when they need a favor." I give her a wide, condescending smile just to piss her off a little more.

"I'm not most people."

I nod. "Agreed, but I have to believe that Vic taught you manners."

"Seriously, you have my hands tied and you're going to play this game?"

I step closer to her, the firmness of her breasts now pushing against my chest. Damn, she feels good and I don't even have a hand on her.

"I can tie you up *and* play games if you like." I raise a brow.

"Ugh. No. I'm not interested in your games."

She says no with those plump lips of hers, but it doesn't escape me that she's still pressed up against me.

"I thought we played pretty nice together. No?"

All I'm able to hear in the darkness is her unsteady breathing—in and out as though it's a struggle.

"I really need to finish this cake so that I can maybe get three hours sleep tonight." Her voice is so low and tense. She's stressed and I'm only adding to that state.

"Say please and it's yours."

"Please, Dane." She even includes my name and by some small miracle, she didn't even use a sarcastic tone.

I click the button and the lights flicker on. Her eyes widen and a genuine smile tugs at her mouth like I just pulled her up on my horse and rode us away from the monsters.

That smile could be addicting.

If you were a different type of guy.

"Thank you." Her hand pats my arm and her chest lets out a long tension filled breath.

"So, Vic did teach you manners?" I smile and step away from her after handing her phone back to her.

"Yes, he did and your dad must have taught you how to fix things." She follows me back out.

She slides by me once we reach the kitchen and starts working again.

"If you keep up this work schedule, you're going to burn out," I say.

A smirk crosses her lips as she looks up at me from the cake she's decorating.

"You're a business owner. I'd think you'd understand."

I jump up on the counter to sit down, and she eyes me for a second but doesn't ask me to leave.

"Who's getting married?"

She scrunches her nose still concentrating on the cake.

"The cake. White tiered cake with buttercream. Wedding?"

She nods, her hands continuing to squeeze the icing onto the cake.

"It's just something to take a picture of so I can use it for promo, show what I can do."

"You're telling me no one is actually going to *eat* that cake?" I hop down from the counter, bending over to get a better look.

She giggles, that heart lightening sound that makes me immediately want to hear it again. "Nope. I need to develop a portfolio, which means, I make and bake them, and they go uneaten."

"That's wasteful." I frown, knowing that cake is way too delicious to go untouched.

"Would you rather I fed it to you?"

"As long as you were naked and we were enjoying it during post-coital bliss." I raise my eyebrows up in a challenge.

She shakes her head. "Do you ever think of anything besides sex?" This time there's no judgment or annoyance in her tone, more like mild curiosity.

"Around you? Not often."

Her cheeks flush the lightest pink, matching the small flowers in the bowl next to the cake.

My phone rings in my pocket and I pull it out.

Shit. The babysitter.

I press the small green button on my screen. "I'll be there in ten. Sorry."

Ashley says it's okay, that Toby is already asleep, but she was concerned because I'm usually home by now.

"Well, I gotta go. My babysitter must have some hot date. Teenagers. Can't keep their hands off each other." She places the icing down on the counter and wipes her hands on an apron that says, 'Every adventure requires a first step.'

"Thank you for your help. I'm worthless in the electrical department."

"You're welcome. Do me a favor though and call an electrician. Norma was supposed to get that fixed. It's happened more than once in the past year." I open the glass door.

"Okay. I'll call in the morning."

I nod and hesitate in the doorway though I have no idea why. "And lock this door after I leave."

She smiles and salutes me. "Yes, Dad."

My gaze tracks every curve of her cute-ass body. She's even sexier when she's covered in flour and icing.

"Oh, I like that. Call me daddy though." This time I can't bite down my laugh.

She shakes her head, laughing lowly and takes my shoulders turning them toward the sidewalk and pushing me out.

"Good night, Dane," she says, and flicks the lock on the door.

I leave knowing that when I picture her underneath me while I'm getting off later, she'll be calling me daddy.

"I love the Alice in Wonderland theme, but I don't think we want to teach the children these sorts of things." Charlie picks up a cookie with Eat Me iced on it.

"Get your mind out of the gutter. There's also Have One and Try Me." I pipe the icing on the last of Dane's cupcakes.

After he had come in like a savior last night, I felt bad I'd pushed off his cupcake order, so I made him an extra dozen with more chocolate shavings than I'd usually use.

"You're practically saying try my pussy and lick my tits. There's sexual innuendos all over these things." She winks and props herself up on the counter, chomping down on an Eat Me cookie. Crumbs fall to her breasts and she brushes them off.

"Um, no. The kids that come in here do not have dirty minds like you." I point my icing tube at her.

"I teach kids about sex for a living. Believe me, the days of using hoo-hah and dinky to describe their private areas are long gone. Kids are growing up fast. Just wait until Lily asks Cat what a cock is."

I laugh, making my icing bag move out of position,

resulting in the icing oozing out and off the cupcake instead of on it. Charlie's gig as a counselor is only part time so she works at Happy Daze to make up the difference.

"Looks like your cupcake pre-ejaculated," she says. "No one likes a dishonorable discharge. Quick shots are for chumps."

"Using the official terms now, huh?" I ask her, grabbing a spatula and wiping the cupcake clean.

I am a professional you know." Charlie raises her shoulders and straightens her back, crossing her legs like she's ready for high tea.

"If Lily ever says cock in front of Marcus, I have to be there. Cat will probably sit her down and explain the whole baby making process while Marcus cries in his office."

We both laugh, but I'm careful this time not to make my cupcake look like it can't hold its icing.

Cat walks in with Lily standing at her side, her big blue eyes on the cookies.

"What's so funny?" Cat asks, grabbing an apron from beside the fridge.

"Nothing. Just thinking how fast kids grow up these days," Charlie comments, grabbing a cookie for Lily and handing it to her.

Lily turns to Cat, and she scrunches her mouth.

"I don't know," she tells Lily, but Lily's puppy dog eyes beg. "Your dad said you're eating too many sweets."

"Here." Charlie hands Lily a Have Me cookie and when I quirk an eyebrow she shrugs. "Safest of the three."

"Fine, but that's it for today though, okay?" Cat's hand brushes down Lily's hair and the two share a look like it's going to be their little secret.

"Mallory said she's coming here today so I'm gonna go wait." Lily takes her cookie and walks out of the kitchen.

Cat fastens her apron behind her back and moves to the sink to wash her hands. "What do you need me to do today?"

I'm not even sure why Cat wants to help so much. I mean, she has her own paintings to work on, but she's been here every day since I opened.

"Um. Can you box these? Charlie's taking them to Dane."

"I think you should deliver them yourself," Charlie says, stealing another cookie from the tray.

"I'm busy." I grab the chocolate chunk and grater.

Charlie looks through the cut-out and back at me. "I don't see people piling in, plus you have a whole glass case full of goodies for people to choose from."

Charlie doesn't take no for an answer easily.

"If it's such a bother for you, I'll just call him to pick them up. I mean I didn't add a delivery charge." Even I know what I'm saying is complete bullshit and the fact that neither of my friends calls me on it, says they're back to assuming something happened with Dane.

"I'm sure he'd love to pick them up." Cat shares a look with Charlie and the two stifle a laugh.

I picture he and I last night and can't help but remember how good he smelled. I had to squeeze my thighs together when he cornered me. I'm not sure I would've objected if he'd tried to kiss me on that sack of flour.

"Bossman took the day off," Charlie says, and the pit of my stomach weighs heavy with disappointment at her words.

Which is ridiculous because what do I care if I won't be seeing Dane Murray today?

"I thought Dane never took a day off?" Cat questions and Charlie shrugs, jumping down from the counter.

"Not unless it's something to do with Toby." She pulls her phone out. "Which reminds me, I need to get to the bar because Toby's coming after school and I get double the pay to watch him until Dane returns." Tucking her phone back in her pocket, she grabs two cookies off the cooling sheet.

"You do know that's how I make a living, right?" I call out to her and her laugh can be heard until the doorbell chimes.

"Seriously, that girl has a bigger sweet tooth than Lily," I comment, finishing up the last cupcake with chocolate shavings. "And she left without taking the cupcakes." I blow out a breath and sit down on my wooden stool, flexing my hands.

Cat secures the lid to the box and taps the bottom. "She did it on purpose."

"Yeah, but if he's not going to be at the bar anyway, then I don't have to rush. She could've mentioned that when she first came."

Cat organizes the boxes and sets them on the completed side, then works on arranging the cookies on a plate.

"Um, Ava, we should keep this G-rated, don't you think?" She holds the cookie up in the air with a smile.

I shake my head. "Both of you have dirty minds, I swear."

She laughs, positioning them on a tray to put out in the glass case. "I'll deliver the cupcakes to Dane once I see his Mustang pull up. No worries." She leaves the kitchen with the tray as I sit there, realizing for the first time how much work this bakery thing really is.

Especially when I'm trying to keep things going because I opened after the summer rush.

An hour later and I've cleaned the entire kitchen

because tonight I promised myself I would snuggle in bed and watch TV until my eyes eventually give out. The after-school rush of parents and their kids have come through already. Cat is sitting with Lily helping her with her homework at a table by the door and other than the soft music I put on over the speakers, there's no other sounds.

I close the blinds to block the sun from streaming in when his car pulls up along the curb. My heart picks up pace, and my hand freezes on the wand of the blinds watching him step out of his sports car.

I'm prepared to see his jeans and t-shirt, my mouth already salivating from the anticipation of seeing how the cotton stretches over his shoulders or how his jeans hang low on his hips. Then a pair of brown dress shoes land on the road and he rises out of the car like an Adonis. I swear every woman in a ten-mile radius senses him. His light brown hair gelled so that every strand is perfectly in place. A crisp white shirt lies under a blue suit jacket and matching blue slacks in a slim fit showcasing how strong his thighs are.

Not that I need to see him in those pants to know how strong they are. I felt them the night he held me up on his lap while he plunged in and out of me.

My body warms from the memory and my pounding heart thuds in my ears.

Standing in the window like an idiot, I don't realize he's swiveling on his dress shoes and heading my way.

"Oh." I back up and run into one of the chairs, circling around until I'm facing Cat and Lily, who are staring at me with concern.

"You okay?" Cat asks, her pencil pausing above the paper she's using to show Lily something.

"Yep. I just forgot I have something to do in the back."

My footsteps increase the closer I get to the kitchen as I race to beat the door chime. By the time I reach the kitchen, I hunch over to catch my breath while searching for something, anything to pull out to look busy. Dane knows no boundaries and he'll see no problem with coming back here.

The door chimes and my stomach ruptures into full-on flight mode.

"Dane!" Cat screams.

Smooth, Cat.

"Uncle Dane!" Lily screeches and I hear the metal chair slide across the floor.

"Hey, Lily. You off from pushing baked goods today?"

The sound of his deep voice is resonating between my thighs.

"Homework." I don't have to be in the room to know she's frowning.

"Well, you don't want to be pushing cupcakes the rest of your life."

Lily giggles.

"What's going on with you?" Cat asks.

"Why? You thinking you picked the wrong single dad?"

I can just picture the cocky expression on his face when he said that.

"Um. Is that an actual question?" I see Cat round the counter and pull his boxes from the bottom shelf.

Okay, yes, I'm spying on them.

"Did Charlie tell you they're ready?" Cat asks.

"What?" he asks, sounding a little confused. If he's not here for the cupcakes why is he here?

The door chimes again. "Who dressed up the monkey?" Marcus chokes out a laugh.

"Daddy!" Lily screeches again, this time a more loving tone.

"Lily Lu," he greets her and I watch Cat's face light up.

"You're not hitting on my girlfriend, are you?" Marcus asks. Dane's just out of my range of view now, but his voice has moved closer.

"You know my number one rule, I don't take what belongs to others." He pauses for a second and I can only see the back of his head so I wonder if he's wearing that panty-melting smirk. "I might have to fight you for the little one though."

"You'll be fighting me for the little one," Cat comments and I assume Marcus is giving her that look that says *you are the perfect woman.*

"Where's the Mad Batter?" Dane asks and I rush over to the fridge, peeking my head in, trying to find something to do. Anything. Seriously, how can I not find one thing out of place? I am not this organized of a person.

"She's working. You know her, the work is never done!" Cat's chipper voice gives me time. If I didn't just scrub down the kitchen, I'd smack a pile of flour all over it.

"I'd like to thank her for the cupcakes."

"Oh yeah, the cupcakes. Is that what they're calling it these days?" Marcus laughs. "Don't you and your happy family have somewhere to be?"

"I'll ring you up and then we're going to dinner," Cat says and then I hear the sound of her pressing buttons on the iPad.

"You guys get going. I'll wait for the Mad Batter to be done. I'm sure she can ring me up."

Cat looks behind her and sees me shaking my head.

"She won't be done for awhile. It's no problem." She presses more buttons.

"So, what happened today?" Marcus asks Dane, and I tiptoe closer to hear their conversation now that their voices are lower.

"Lily, pack up your bag. We'll finish at home," Cat calls out over their conversation and I grit my teeth.

"It just takes time. Though I might as well hand them my checkbook between all the fees," Dane says to Marcus.

"It's for the best though, right?" Marcus says back.

"Yeah, but..." Cat decides to open the cash drawer and since I bought it at a restaurant salvage store, it's clunky and loud and now I can't hear shit.

"I never knew you could clean up so well." Marcus laughs, and Cat starts untying her apron.

"I'll be right back," she says.

She appears in the kitchen doorway, her eyebrows raised at my ear perched to the wall.

"Hmm." She takes the apron off her neck and hangs it up by the fridge.

"What?" I whisper, my hands going up in the air.

"Nothing." The smirk says it's something. "So, Ava, I'm heading out for the night." She speaks loud enough so everyone in the place can hear her.

I tilt my head and roll my eyes at her. "Thanks for the help."

She pats my arm. "Anytime. Go home and get some sleep tonight."

"I will."

She leaves the kitchen and I hear Marcus and Dane talking until the door chimes.

Finally, the tension in my body drains and I sit on the stool, contemplating why I care so much and contemplating why Dane in a suit resulted in the same reaction as if Chris Evans had walked into my store.

Shaking my head and forcing myself not to think about it any longer, I stand to leave, but he appears in the doorway —his sunglasses hanging off the pocket of his suit jacket, his shoulder leaning on the doorframe, ankles crossed.

"Dane."

"I'm getting déjà vu when you say my name so breathlessly." His cocky smirk is in place and though I usually want to smack it off his face, this time I find myself wanting to kiss it off.

Fuck, stop it, Ava.

"Funny. What can I do for you?" I ask. My fingers need something to do so they knot together in my lap.

"I wanted to thank you for the cupcakes."

I nod. "You're welcome."

"A whole dozen for free. I should repay you."

With his mouth?

Crap. No Ava. Stop it.

"Not necessary. Thanks for your help last night." I nod, my comebacks not nearly as snappy as they should be.

"Any man would love to be a girl's knight in shining armor." He winks and my heart skips a beat or two before I think of something to say back.

"Well, I wouldn't go that far. I'm not afraid of the dark." I grab my purse from the counter. If I leave, he leaves and then I can pull myself together and remind myself why Dane Murray is not the man I want to be with.

"You closing up early tonight?" He's pushed off the wall now, his stance wider, blocking my way out of the kitchen as he plays with his sunglasses in his hands.

"Yeah. If I don't sleep soon, I'm going to collapse." I turn off the lights in the back.

He steps to the side, extending his arm out for me to go

first in an exaggerated movement. I wait for him to grab the three pink boxes of cupcakes, which he does with ease.

Well, Ava, he lifts kegs of beer on the daily.

"Then I'll try not to invade too much." I open the door and he steps out, his sunglasses in his free hand about to cover his eyes.

"What?" I ask, the door still in my hands.

"I'll try not to invade your dreams too much tonight." He winks, puts his sunglasses on and turns around. "Sweet dreams, Ava, or rather, dirty dreams."

I immediately look right and left to see if anyone is close by. Phew, no one.

His laugh rings out as he crosses the street and disappears into his bar. He must have a game plan and I need to figure it out if I'm going to stay one step ahead of him.

7

DANE

It's Saturday morning, and Toby came to the bar with me because he wants to earn some extra money for the new Xbox football game he's been begging me for. He's washing the tables down while I sit at the table reserved for my dad and his friends, although, they haven't been coming as much lately. Probably because they'd don't agree with the grill.

I shake my head recalling the conversation when I originally wanted to get permits to open a restaurant alongside the bar. He never understood why the bar wasn't good enough, but I knew there was an opportunity for growth with how much the tourist season had increased. I mean we've opened more bed and breakfasts, and I might not agree with it, but large hotel chains have inquired about opening up in town. Town council will never let that happen.

"Can we order it tonight?" Toby asks, spraying down another table and chairs.

He is a hard worker, I'll give him that.

"We have your game first."

The phone rings and I walk over to the counter to grab it.

"Happy Daze," I answer.

"Dane?" Norma, the previous owner of the bakery's shaky voice will always be recognizable to me. Hell, she's been my cookie supplier since I was two.

"Miss Sawyer. How is Arizona?"

I tuck the phone under my chin and sign a few papers from the beer distributors that needed my attention.

"Oh, it's nice but I miss Climax Cove. Hey, dear, I had a question for you."

"Sure. I always have time for my pseudo-grandma."

She giggles and then starts coughing.

"You okay?"

She clears her throat, and I grab hold of the phone to pull it away from my ear. I'd rather not lose my hearing today.

"Yes. Sorry." Another clearing of her throat. "The girl that took over the bakery…"

"Ava?"

"Yes, Ava. How does it seem business is going?"

That's sweet she's worried about her.

"I guess it's good. She's changed the whole thing into an Alice in Wonderland theme."

"Oh, nice. Well, she's late on her payment. I wanted to make sure she was still in business."

Damn it. I knew her opening right after summer wasn't the wisest decision, but Ava isn't one to take advice from others.

"Could you not call her?" I ask.

See, this is what people find wrong with a small town. I shouldn't know about Ava's payment being late, it's none of my business. The gossip mill has thinned out as the cemeteries have grown, but it will never truly die off.

"I don't want to stress her out. To be honest I was nervous letting her take over the business on a payment plan rather than buying outright, but what choice did I have? It's a small town and she was the only person that showed any interest. She's a good girl and I think she's good for the money, I just wanted to make sure it was open."

"And why am I your first call?"

If things have already hit the mill about Ava and me, then we have spies around here.

"You're across the street."

I cock my head. "Makes sense."

"Well, I have to take my sister to the doctor."

"I hope all is well there?"

She laughs, spurring another coughing fit. "Yes. Things here are nice. Please don't say anything to Ava, I would hate for her to feel like we're talking about her."

I refrain from the smart-ass comment I could say back.

"Sure thing."

"I'm sure business will pick up for her." I hear shuffling on the other end. "We need to leave. I'll talk to you soon. Bye, Dane."

The line clicks dead before I can respond. I press the off button and my gaze shifts over to the window so I can see across the street.

The sun is shining today and Ava's moved a few of the tables out onto the sidewalk. Her door is open and I see her preparing to open inside by sliding those delicious crack cakes—that's what I'm calling her cupcakes now—into the glass case.

"What are you doing?" Toby pulls me out of my daze and I look back to find his eyebrows raised.

"Nothing." I stand up, grabbing the phone to put on the base.

"You were staring at Miss Ava."

"No, I wasn't." I crinkle my eyes to throw off his scent.

"You were bent over on the bar, staring."

Of course, he can't leave well enough alone.

"Are you done?" I ask.

Parenting tip—always distract.

"Yeah. So, did I earn the money for the game yet?"

"Take that spray and rag into the back. Then we need to get you changed for your baseball game."

He smiles taking my answer as a yes. I can't complain, he's a good kid and if he wants a video game, it's the least I can do.

My gaze veers out the window again, but Toby rushes out a second later, his uniform in his hands, so I shift my gaze his way.

"Ready?" I ask.

"Yeah. Carter totally rocked first base at the last game," Toby says.

I ruffle his hair and nod to the bathroom to change. "And put your clothes in a neat pile to change into later," I call out.

His response to my directions is to shut the door.

With Toby in the bathroom and no one else in the bar since we're not open yet, I stand at the window, like a stalker, watching her smile as she stands with samples on the sidewalk. Her long hair is pulled back into a ponytail and her jeans are form fitting, but today she has red Chucks on, rather than her usual black ones. I notice a bicycle chained to the bike holder in front of Nail Me Hardware store beside her shop and I realize I've never contemplated whether she has a car.

"Dad!" Toby's voice startles me and I turn so fast, I pull a neck muscle.

"What?" I ask, cringing.

"Let's go. We can't be late."

"Go to the car, I'll be right out." I scribble down a note for my parents who are opening until I get back from the game, swipe my keys from the counter, and head out.

I lock up the doors to the bar, wave to Ava, without my eyes staying on her too long and slide into my car with Toby who's voicing his concern that we're going to be late. The kid does not get his worrying from me. Must be his mom...strike that. I have no clue where he gets it from.

THE CLIMAX COVE RAIDERS WIN TWELVE TO EIGHT.

Toby orders his video game on my phone on the ride back to the bar. There are times I feel bad for how much time Toby has to spend at the bar and grill. The small arcade I installed doesn't fill up his time unless one of his friends comes in with their family for dinner. Then usually the parents love it because the boys will go off and play while they have a quiet meal.

But at this point in the bar's financials, I have no choice. I haven't found anyone other than Charlie that I trust enough not to screw me over.

"Grandma is going to take you home tonight," I tell him and I see his frown from my rearview mirror.

"Hey, tomorrow is all us, buddy. Rafting."

His frown instantly turns into a smile. "Last one for the season, right?" His eyes meet mine in the mirror.

"We'll see, maybe we can get out again soon."

"Are Uncle Garrett and Sydney coming this time?"

"No, it's just us."

His smile grows wider, and I know it's not because he doesn't like Garrett and his daughter Sydney, but since the grill opened, he hasn't had enough time with just me.

I pull into the back alleyway since the street will be busy today with it being Saturday. Toby climbs out and runs inside the back door. I follow behind, leaving all his stuff in the trunk since we'll be back on the ballfield in two days.

My mom is hovered over the stove with Toby by her side now, the wooden spoon at his lips.

"What are you doing?" I ask, greeting her myself with a kiss on the cheek.

"I thought you'd like a batch of my sauce. You can freeze some and serve it for a special or something." She smiles and places the spoon that was just in Toby's mouth on the resting plate.

As she scoops pasta she's already made into a bowl for Toby, I take the spoon and toss it in the sink, replacing it with a new one. Sometimes my mom doesn't understand that she's not cooking Sunday dinner for our family.

"Thanks, Mom."

Where my dad hated the idea of adding a grill to the bar, my mom helped me come up with a good menu and is always willing to help me out.

"Dad in the front?" I ask.

She spoons the sauce into Toby's dish and then pulls up a chair next to her. "Sit and tell me about your game."

Toby smiles, never one not to want to replay each game with anyone who asks.

Leaving them to their grandma and grandson bonding time, I escape into my office and switch my now dust covered gym shoes to a clean pair.

Walking down the hallway, I pause finding my dad behind the bar, sitting on a stool, talking with his friends.

The bar isn't horribly busy, but people are starting to find their way into town now.

"Thanks, Dad, I got it from here." I pat his back, circle around him and ask the first person what they'd like to drink.

"You need help. I always had help."

"You had me and Sara," I deadpan, not in the mood for another lecture today. Nothing I do is good enough for him.

"Yeah. Help."

He walks out from behind the bar, to his table in the back. His friends swivel off their stools to join him. In between serving drinks, I grab the stool, and place it back on the other side of the bar.

I hate asking for help, especially from my father, but Toby was way too excited for me to coach his Little League fall team.

"Hey, Dane. Do we have cupcakes?" Aurora, one of my servers asks me.

"No. Who's asking?" I look into the seating area.

"They said they were here the other night and you served chocolate ones or something?

"Oh, that was a trial. So, they want another one?"

"I'm guessing so since they're asking," she says, thick with sarcasm. Aurora and her smart mouth. She's just returned from college after failing out her freshman year. I was hesitant to hire her but other than her mouth, she's a hard worker.

"Stall them, I'll be right back."

I tell Matt, my part-time server slash bartender slash fireman, I'll be back in a minute.

Jogging across the street, I'm happy to find that Mad

Batter has a few people milling around. Although, I'd like to see a million different pink boxes walking out the bakery door.

I step behind the counter and swing the kitchen door open, finding Ava icing another batch of cupcakes.

"What kind are those?" I ask, leaning against the doorframe.

Icing squeezes out all over her table.

"Has anyone ever explained boundaries to you?"

I pause acting as though I'm thinking. "Usually women like it when I bypass their boundaries."

Her face scrunches up in a *give me a break look* and she rolls her eyes. "How can I help you, Dane?"

"Well, now that you ask." I step into the kitchen and her gaze stays on me the entire time. I prop myself up on her counter, watching her scoop more frosting into her bag. "I have a business proposition for you."

That perfect ass of hers falls onto the stool she always keeps nearby and I'm guessing her legs get as tired as mine do from standing all day.

"If you haven't noticed, I have a business."

I purposely glance around the store. "I can see that. I want you to make cupcakes for me for the restaurant."

Her hazel eyes narrow. "Wouldn't that take business away from me? You are right across the street."

I grab a cookie from the baking sheet and hold it up to read it. "Try Me?" I raise a brow. "You know all you have to do is say the word." I wink.

Her scowl diminishes as pink tints her cheeks.

"I see you're not in a laughing mood today, so I'll cut to the chase. You supply me with one type of cupcake, ones you don't sell here. I'll credit you on our menus and I'll make sure my staff tells everyone where they're from.

Believe me, after one, they'll be coming across the street for more. It's a win-win."

She places the icing on the table. If she's as strapped as Mrs. Sawyer implied, she'll take the bait. Honestly, this will help both of us.

"Okay, we can try it out." She stands to her feet, grabs her icing and starts frosting the cupcakes again.

"So, right now, I need two dozen of something."

She scoffs. "I thought this was a 'we'll talk more in the future' type thing?"

I round my wrist up. "Time's a ticking. I have a table who wants your cupcakes right now."

She looks around the table. There's way more than she'll sell today, but I'm not a moron, I'm not telling her that.

"You can take these." She shuffles over to her shelves, rising on her tiptoes to grab the box.

"Here." I jump off the counter, and reach above her, grabbing the box for her.

She turns and I see this isn't the best position for two people who just went into business together. I'm not sure I'll ever grow tired of watching her chest rise and fall with deep breaths when she's in close proximity to me though.

I back away and her hands hurriedly try to fill the box.

"What kind are these?" I ask, filling the second box for her.

"Salted caramel." She closes the box, fastens it and then slides it my way.

"How much?" I pull out my wallet.

"Just take those and we'll come up with a plan when you have more time."

I stack the two boxes on top of each other and pick them up. "So, you're going to agree to spend more time with me?"

She gives me that exasperated look again. "For business, yes."

"You book the taste test and let me know."

She nods, her hands landing on my sides, swiveling me around toward the door.

"Now, go. I need to wrap my brain around the fact that I'm desperate enough to invite you into my life everyday." Her voice is light, casual, and full of sarcasm.

"Most ladies find me a pleasure to be with."

Her hands haven't left my back as she follows me to the doorway.

"I never have been a go-with-the-crowd kinda gal."

I chuckle, turning around and her hands slide around my entire stomach. Damn her touch feels good.

"I think I need to refresh your memory on how pleasurable I can be."

She rolls her eyes, but she can't bite her lip enough to stop that smile. The smile that jumbles my stomach into a what-the-fuck-is-going-on ruckus.

"Bye, Dane." She lightly pushes me out the kitchen door.

"Pleasure doing business with you." I wink again and she shakes her head, turning around to go back to her decorating while I walk through her store, wondering what I just got myself into.

8

AVA

I closed the shop early because it's Sunday and no one was really around since the town one over was having their annual fall festival. Next year, I need to grab a booth to sell my stuff and see if I can draw in some locals from neighboring towns.

The warm sun soaks into my skin and I close my eyes as the fresh air breezes by me. I hadn't realized how long it was since I spent time outside and not inside a hot kitchen with sugar and eggs as my only companions.

"I can squeeze you in on the next one if that's okay?" The hot ass tour guide at the rafting company approaches me.

"Oh, great. Definitely okay."

He smiles this double dimple megawatt grin that brings girls to their knees asking him for the pleasure of sucking him off, I'm sure. Under normal circumstances, I'd probably spend the rest of my day flirting with him in the hopes he'd ask me out by sunset. But not today. Today is a solo day, which means it's all about me.

"Go grab a vest." He practically flexes his muscles while

he points to the post with all the jackets hanging. "Chill out for a bit, and they'll call you when they're ready." Again, with the smile. Yep, this guy rarely gets turned down from girls.

"Thanks," I look at his nametag, "Bradley."

"Brad." He corrects me, shrugging those big shoulders he must work on daily at the gym. While the girls drool on the ellipticals, I'm sure.

Sorry dreamboat, today isn't the day.

"Thanks." I walk over to pick out my jacket.

Brad moves behind the counter to continue helping the people who already had reservations. Sometimes it's a benefit to be a party of one.

Sitting on a rock by the river, I absorb the serenity the wilderness always gives me, watching the rafting boats come in and out, most filled with families. I could have asked my dad to come with me today, but he'll want to gush on about how proud he is of me, or how happy he is I decided to stay in Climax Cove. Right now, I want to forget all the pressure of the bakery, all the expectations my dad or the town has.

Shaking my head, I try to rid my mind of all the stresses and enjoy a day I rarely get.

I strip off my yoga pants leaving me in my swim shorts hoping to not lose what's left of my tan from the summer.

"Miss Ava!" a kid screams and I turn around, my eyes taking in a boy with a mop of hair running toward me.

His footsteps skid to a stop on the dirt and gravel once he's near.

"Toby! What a surprise."

Please tell me your grandparents brought you, or maybe that babysitter.

"Well, looky looky, it's the Mad Batter."

No such luck.

My gaze skirts to Dane, slowly walking toward us. Good to know he wears his shorts like he does his pants, low. That groin cleavage lays there under his white t-shirt just waiting for an unsuspecting female victim to come along.

"Dad, it's Miss Ava."

"Yeah." He stops next to his son, his hand landing on his shoulder. "I see her." He eyes my bare legs and I curl them into my body as though I can hide them. "Rafting?"

I'm so focused on the goose bumps on my skin from his assessing eyes, it takes a minute for my brain to process the words he just spoke. "I'm sorry?"

He chuckles and then sucks his lips in to stop the laughter while Toby looks back and forth between us.

"Rafting? Are you rafting today, Miss Ava?" Toby's wide eyes and smile full of missing teeth would make me say yes even if I wasn't.

"Yes."

He hops on the rock next to me. "So are my dad and me! I'm so excited." He strips off his t-shirt and then fastens his life jacket over his chest.

Dane picks up the shirt, folding it and placing it in his backpack.

Please don't take off your t-shirt. Please don't take off your t-shirt.

He's taking off his shirt.

Dane's hands reach for the hem of his t-shirt and I'm still repeating the chant in my head, but it does no good. Instead, he removes the piece of clothing revealing what he's most proud of—his perfect V.

"Do you need a water?" he asks.

My eyes flick to his face and that cocky smirk is in place as always.

Not waiting for me to answer, he continues. "You just look so flushed. Maybe too much time in the sun?"

I stare at him unamused until I remember we're not in the back of my shop bantering with no witnesses. Toby is right next to me, so I detour my attention to him.

"What's your favorite part of rafting?" I ask.

He smiles, clearly happy that I'm granting him some of my attention. "Dad won't let me go on any crazy white water yet, but I love paddling."

I glance back at Dane, who shakes his head, obviously a constant point of stress in their household.

"You're eight," he says.

Toby's jaw drops open as he stares at Dane. "Jack was six when his parents took him out."

"Jack's a liar," Dane says straight-faced. "I'm grabbing drinks. Either of you?" He points back and forth.

"No thanks," I say.

"Gatorade for me. Orange!" Toby screams, and Dane doesn't bother turning around.

Brad approaches us on the rock. "Miss Pearson, we're all set for you. You'll be on that one." He points to a group of guys all climbing into a raft.

"I'm sorry. The one with all the men?" I ask to clarify and Toby and I share a look of I'm-not-so-sure-about-this.

"It's a bachelor party, but they haven't been drinking."

So much for a solo day.

"Peachy." I stand up, grab my yoga pants and start putting them on. "I'll be right there."

"You're going to go with all of them?" Toby asks, his bottom lip pushed out a little more than normal.

"Well, I didn't call ahead so it's the only raft they can fit me on." I smile down and Toby shifts his eyes to the boat and then to me. "Why don't you come on our boat?"

What am I supposed to say? That I want the white water rafting experience and not the sail down a calm river paddling.

"That's the one they assigned me to."

Toby still looks confused. I have one leg in my yoga pants when Dane approaches, his gaze not missing the fact that I'm dressing.

"Dad, Miss Ava is going on that boat." He points, and we all follow the direction of his finger to the group of guys currently seeing who can hit the other one harder.

"Them? They look like a bunch of gym rats."

"I already told Toby, I don't have a reservation, so it's the only boat that has room for me." Why am I making excuses? This is none of their business.

"Well, Toby, say goodbye to Miss Ava." Dane steps out of the way for me to get down from the rock.

"But, Dad...." Toby whines, but Dane seems happy I'm leaving.

Why does that irk me?

"Maybe we'll see her after." Dane's gaze shifts to the raft where the guys are now staring over at us. "I'm sure there won't be any time for them to get too handsy," he whispers, and I jolt back, staring him straight in the eye.

A smirk edges the corner of his lips and my gaze instinctively moves down his torso.

"You always were a fan of my cleavage." He raises his eyebrows up in a challenge.

I take a deep breath and purposely keep my gaze directed in front of me as I walk away. I'm almost to the raft, hearing the guys razzing others about me riding along with them. Do I really want to endure this just to prove a point to Dane?

I'm running out of time when the guy in the front, the one with the loud mouth and the biggest muscles bends over and throws up in the raft. My feet stop.

"Fuck man!" one friend says.

"Get off the raft." The guide points to the dock. "You're done for the day." Turning their attention to me the guide continues. "I'm sorry, ma'am, we'll have to clean it out and disinfect it."

My head falls back in defeat, and I glance over my shoulder, finding Dane's know-it-all smirk more prominent than before. Asshole.

The next thing I know, Brad's standing next to me, his dimples now hidden under a mask of annoyance.

"Sorry Miss Pearson. I'll look to see if we have anything else."

I follow him back to the counter, and he's checking clipboards, looking between one sheet and another.

"I can get you on the slower tour, but not the white water." He drops the clipboard, and his shoulders fall.

Either that or nothing.

"I'll come back another day," I say.

"Okay, but there's no refunds." Smiley Brad points to the sign etched in wood.

"But, this is out of my control.," I point out.

"Doesn't matter." He shrugs. "We'll offer you a ride on the family raft and give you a coupon for your inconvenience. That's our policy." He holds out the coupon.

"Seriously?" I ask, still not believing they won't give me back my money or at the very least reschedule me.

"Sorry, but yep."

I changed my mind. I don't know how Brad gets any of the girls because Brad is a big, dumb jerk.

I grab the coupon out of his hand and spin on my heels, coming face to face with Dane.

Shit.

9

DANE

I'm unsure if Ava is part of some dick punishing mission, but after she got stuck on our raft, she stripped down to her tight swim shorts and tank swim top. Thankfully, her tits are covered and her top covers the strip of flat stomach invisible to everyone else. I still get tormented thinking of the small patch of dark hair right above her pussy.

"Miss Ava," Toby takes the seat next to her, leaving me to sit on the other side of him. "This is going to be so much fun!" Toby's wide eyes volley between me and her and I hope the kid isn't thinking something crazy like Marcus and Garrett. I know he's missed out on having a mom and he doesn't always understand why his didn't stick around, but I'm not built for a long-lasting relationship.

She smiles, but I see her hesitancy in sharing this day with us. Hell, I had been looking forward to it being just me and Toby, too.

"Here." I hold my hand out to take her yoga pants and t-shirt she has shoved on the floor of the raft.

"It's okay." She shakes her head like the bullheaded, stubborn woman she is.

"Just give them to me."

Toby reaches down, grabs them and hands them to me.

"They'll get wet," he tells her, and the smile she always has on call for him shines through.

"Thanks," she says it more to Toby than me, but I unzip my backpack and shove them in with our clothes.

Before we can talk any further, our tour guide hops on board with his sunglasses and million-dollar smile. I know the owner of the rafting company and he has a very specific hiring pattern. Illegal or not, no one over thirty-five gets a shot. Looking at his time clock hitters today, I'd say it's more likely that thirty is the cut-off. All good-looking guys, sprinkled with a couple girls probably for the bachelor party groups. Hopefully, they don't kill us.

"Hey, I'm Cameron, and I'm your guide for the day. We're going to start off slow, but we'll go through a few rougher patches." He looks down at the family right in front of him, the mom now looking from her husband to their five-year-old. "No worries, ma'am, no one has ever fallen out on my tour."

I roll my eyes, there's a first time for everything buddy, and now you just jinxed us.

"Okay then, everyone received their instructions on shore. Any more questions?" he asks. When no one speaks, up he continues, "Let's get going. Parents you're doing the paddling. I'll just make my way to the back."

He jumps on the deck and then rounds the back of the raft.

"Can't I go on the edge?" Toby whines and before Ava was joining us I had planned to let him this once, but we need the adults with the paddles.

"It's a class three."

"Dad?" he whines and I can't blame the kid. I'm fairly sure it's my family genes that gave him his rebellious live on the edge mentality.

"After first break. Okay? Then I'll let you in front of me and I'll move to the back." I nod my head to where there's an empty spot right in front of the guide.

Toby smiles big and nods. "Awesome."

His own enjoyment fills me with happiness. Nothing like your kid being happy.

Then I glance behind him, finding Ava's lips upturned staring at the two of us. Once she discovers I've caught her, she focuses forward and prepares her paddle.

The first part of the trip isn't that bad and it's more serene and for enjoying the sounds of nature and discovering the world we live in. Nothing is better than being outside and that's why I never had an urge like my sister did to disappear to the big city. I love campouts when summer is right on the cusp of ending. When you're sweating during the day, but chilly at night for a campfire. I love grabbing my bike and heading to the hills to lose myself in my thoughts and enjoy the thrill of following an unpaved track. Yeah, I could live on the beach down in California or on the east coast, but there's nothing better than sitting on my deck with the trees surrounding me as I stare out over never-ending water.

"We're about to come to some small dips, so you young-sters don't go jumping," Cameron warns.

I look to Toby who's bored out of his mind. He wants to use the paddle in his hand, and he wants to experience the adventure. After we get through the dips, I look back to Cameron, currently basking in the sun.

"Hey, we're going to swap." I point to Toby whose eyes

light up with excitement. "Just remember what I taught you. The last thing I want is to have to show off my savior skills in front of Ava." I wink at her, knowing she's observing us. Her gaze has been nailed to us almost the entire trip.

She quickly turns around, embarrassed I caught her...again.

"Sure thing. We're on calm water for a few." Cameron's head falls back again.

I slide back onto the other plank and Toby slides into my empty spot, propping his butt on the edge of the raft.

"Now, Toby, when we dip down you lift the paddle," I start instructing him, but he places his hand in the air. "If you'd rather go back to twiddling your thumbs." My words are meant to threaten him.

He shakes his head. "No. I got it, Dad."

To even out the weight of the boat, I'm stuck in the middle of the last row, twiddling my thumbs and giving me nothing else to do but keep an eye on Toby.

"Okay, hope you're ready young guns, we're heading toward the class three river."

Toby looks over his shoulder to me, a fear that wasn't there moments ago emerging.

"You got this." I wink and he smiles and then sets his gaze forward.

I try to calm down my pounding heartbeat watching the falls appear in the distance. What is probably seconds long feels like an hour until the top of the raft falls and all of us slide down. Toby does awesome like I thought he would, but another one comes immediately, and we plunge.

"Toby, paddle." I give him directions and his arms go strong.

Ava's helping out by paddling double speed, thank goodness.

"Everyone stop," Cameron calls out when we get to a calmer spot. He directs his bigger paddles into the water to maneuver the boat a certain direction down the river.

We fall into a dip in the surge and a huge wave of water drenches us.

"Go, go," he says, and Toby paddles his heart out.

I wasn't prepared for one slip after the other, and I bite down screaming directions at Toby. Soon my eyes stop looking at what's coming and I focus completely on him. I still treat him like a child but look at him manning up and handling a class three river.

He breaks when he needs to, propels the raft when it's required, and the best part is his gaze never veers from where we're headed. My heart warms and I probably look like a goon smiling over at him.

Finally, the raft is gliding and all of Toby's teeth—what he hasn't lost and been richly rewarded for by the Tooth Fairy—are smiling back at me.

"Okay group, we're going to tie up over to the left." Cameron points to a clearing where I'm guessing the rafting company has a snack area.

Toby straightens his back and helps his group out by doing his share of the paddling.

Once we reach the rest area and we're out of the raft, I wrap my arm around his neck, pulling him into my chest.

"You did fantastic!" His face flushes and he tries to toss off my compliment. "I'm serious. Have you been going out without me?"

He laughs, shaking his head. "No," he mumbles.

"I'm really proud of you." I rub my knuckles on his head and pull him to my side where he stands limp and he shoves off my praise again.

Toby's a lot like me. We love attention, but never when

we do something good or when someone is proud of us. That's when expectations are born.

"So, I can do class four now?"

Ava laughs and I realize I almost forgot she was with us. I search her out, finding her right behind me. She appears mesmerized by the scene in front of her and I'm not sure why.

"We'll talk about it, but let's master class three for awhile."

Toby squirms out of my arm hold, stalking off to the snack table. He's struggling to fight the smile on his face, which makes me grin.

"Who would have guessed?" Ava says, then sashays by me.

"What?"

"That there's actually one person in this world who has the power to shut you up."

She smiles over her shoulder and continues on her way to the snack table.

An urge spurs inside me to bend her over my knee and smack that fine round ass, but instead, I follow behind.

"Well, I don't know about that. Your cupcakes can shut me up." I fall into line with her, both of us walking toward Toby and the snack table. "Which brings up the subject of my taste test."

I feel her eyes on me, but I keep mine straight ahead so I don't seem too eager.

"How about tomorrow night. Monday's are usually dead for you, right?"

This earns my attention, and I turn to look down at her. "For someone who acts like she can't stand the sight of me, you sure seem to keep tabs on me. You got a set of binoculars over there in your shop?"

She stares at me blankly until she has no choice but to face forward or risk tripping on a root.

"It's not that I can't stand the sight of you, it's just that you're everything that's bad for me."

I cup her elbow, quickly guiding her over to a more secluded area. Cameron is busy talking to Toby who's nodding at him while chewing his granola bar.

"Bad for you?" What the hell is she talking about?

Truth be told, I've shared two nights with Ava against my better judgment. Don't get me wrong, both nights she rocked my world more than anyone I've ever been with. But she was still the daughter of an acquaintance of mine. Vic rolls by the bar for the odd Single Dads Club meetings. But when I brought it up that second night in my office she reminded me that she's an adult and is free to make her own decisions. She's right, I know she is, but it did take some convincing on her part. Lucky for me, Ava is really good at convincing when she uses her mouth.

Those two encounters have stayed with me. Especially, since one was in my bedroom and I swore even after I washed the sheets, her scent still lingered. Second time, was in my office. Talk about shitting where you eat. This is like fucking where you live. Now visions of her spread eagle on my desk embed my vision every time I'm in my office at the bar and when I lay down at night. I remember the feeling of having her pussy on my mouth as she straddled my face.

"Yes. I thought I could do the whole screw-you-when-ever, but I just can't do that knowing that you're out messing around with other people."

"That's why you dodged me after the time in my office?"

She nods, her eyes studying whatever the fuck is over my shoulder.

"Ava." My hand reaches out, but I retract it because I

don't want to ruin the friendship we've started. Friendship might not be the best word, but at least she no longer hates me. "I never meant to disrespect you."

She shakes her head, dismissing my words. When she finally looks me in the eye, it's there, what I somehow always knew was there—she's not like the other girls I usually get with. The ones who aren't looking for something beyond a night or two.

"*I* let you disrespect me. *I* came to the bar that night. We both knew what I wanted and it wasn't your hand in marriage."

"But?"

"But it's not me. The whole friends-with-benefits is one thing. The last thing I want is a boyfriend. I've got enough going on right now trying to get this business off the ground."

"Phew," I slip out.

Her gaze bounces over to me once again, her soft smile fading.

"I also can't be one of many and I was upset with you when I had no reason to be. We made no promises, but I changed my mind afterward."

"So, we can be friends?" I ask, not arguing the point.

Ava's sexy as hell and my dick is in full chub mode when she's near, but I don't do monogamy even when it's friends with benefits.

"Why do you want to be friends?" She scrunches her eyebrows.

I chuckle. "Listen, if we're going to be business owners across the street from one another, I think we need to be civil at the very least. You seem like a fun girl and I'm a fun guy. Too bad we can't enjoy each other's company now and then, but hey, I promise not to touch if you do," I waggle my eyebrows.

Finally, that soft smile that's teetered on the edge of gloom goes full wattage and she nods.

"Friends." She shrugs like it's no sweat off her back.

"If I cop a feel once in awhile, that's okay, right?" I joke, walking past her and toward the snack table.

She turns and walks beside me.

"As long as you don't mind a knee in the nuts."

I scoff. "You wouldn't."

"Touch and see." She quirks an eyebrow issuing a challenge.

"You scare me."

She laughs and if only that sound didn't spur a spark of something in my stomach, then I'd be absolutely certain that I could be friends with a girl for once in my life.

Taste test! What was I thinking? I should've sent the samples over with Charlie earlier today. She would have handed them to him, and he could test them out alone in his office.

But no, I had to go ahead and agree to be *friends* with him. Then I agreed to have him at the shop after hours to taste test a few cupcakes he might want to serve at Happy Daze.

Yeah, long story short, I'm a moron.

Admitting my feelings to him at the water rafting excursion wasn't in the plan. My plan when I left his bar that next morning after falling asleep on the couch in his office was to act indifferent. To never let him know how he hurt me after seeing the text from his date the night before.

I'm not sure what woke me up, but I slithered out from under the blanket I was sharing with Dane. The leather couch crinkled and I stopped, waiting until I saw his steady breathing. With him still asleep, I tiptoed around the room, scooping up my clothes that Dane had stripped off me the night before after I'd shown up thirsty for more than just a drink at his bar.

I watched him sleep, a beautiful man that used his good looks to lure women. Who am I judging? It worked on me. Twice now.

After shrugging my shirt over my head, his phone dinged on the desk.

A picture of him and a woman crossed the screen with a caption, 'Be careful I bite'.

I picked up his phone thinking I'd be able to see more and be able to tell who the hell the woman was, but his password screen came up, so, I did what any normal female would, I stalked him on Instagram.

It didn't take long to find the picture linked to his profile. I'm not sure the man holds any secrets.

Pollyanna or whatever her name was, had her cheek pressed against his. He was wearing the same clothes that I just stepped over, so unless I'm an even bigger moron, he went from her to me last night. Hours before he bent me over his desk, he was with her.

That's when I knew, this casual sex thing wasn't for me. I'm not built to share a man. So, I took one last look at Dane knowing that whatever we were doing was over and prayed that neither of my roommates would be up when I tried to slip in our apartment unseen.

What's that saying? Fool me once shame on you. Fool me twice, and I'm an idiot who needs to stay far, far away from Dane Murray.

A light tap sounds on the window of my door and my heart rate picks up speed. I ignore the temptation to glance in a mirror. To straighten my ponytail or make sure the lip gloss I applied minutes ago is still on.

Walking through the front part of the shop, seeing his smiling face behind the glass, warms my stomach.

I unlock the door and push it open. "Hey."

"Glad to see you listened to me last time and kept the

door locked." He slides in through the opening, locking it behind him.

"Yeah, you'd never want that robber with the late night sweet tooth to break in."

I walk toward the back. The sooner we get it going, the sooner it's over.

I reach the kitchen and plate the samples while Dane slides onto the stool next to me.

He's wearing cologne tonight. God, it makes him smell so good.

It's probably for a date. Probably for one of his bang buddies.

Block it out. Block it out.

Be professional.

I push the plate toward him. I do my best not to divert my gaze between his wide-open legs. My mind tries not to remember the length and girth of what lies under those jeans. My pussy tries not to throb with the memory of how he filled me up.

She's doing a really shitty job in that department.

"So, what do we have here?" he asks.

I back up to sit on my own stool, attempting to create some distance between us.

"I stuck with a drink theme so they're all based on alcoholic drink flavors. Like margarita and strawberry daiquiri."

His fingers wrap around the Kailua and crème cupcake and he holds it up to his nose and smells it.

"A dessert cupcake." He smiles and a pair of hands have never looked more appetizing to me as he peels back the paper. If the hands weren't enough to turn my thermostat on high, watching his mouth open and his perfectly white teeth bite into my creation, has me practically waving myself to cool down.

Why is that such a turn on?

An enjoyable mumble rumbles out of him and he closes his eyes briefly as he chews and swallows.

I cross my legs to tame the fire his noises ignited.

"Put a ring on it." He shakes his head in disbelief.

"What?" I giggle like a schoolgirl.

Stop it.

"The cupcake, all your cupcakes. So. Fucking. Good."

He peruses the other ones, his eyes widening as he takes them all in.

"Which one should I choose?" His hand floats over the tray until he picks up the sangria one.

"That's a sangria berry flavored."

His smile grows. "Perfect. You really picked some great samples here."

Again, my breathing hitches, my heart thumps in my chest watching him eat another cupcake.

He reacts the same, eyes closed, inaudible murmur and I force myself to stay seated instead of straddling him and inviting him to eat the cupcakes off my naked body.

Real professional, Ava.

We continue this torture for another four cupcakes until Dane pushes the tray to the side.

"I think I've indulged enough and I can confidently say, you can make whatever the hell you want for my grill." He pats his stomach. "Damn, girl, where did you learn to bake?"

Needing to escape the closeness of us, I grab two waters from the fridge and hand him one.

His forearms flex as he twists it open and his Adam's apple bobs when he guzzles down half the bottle. "Thanks."

I nod.

"So, where did you learn?" He turns his body on the stool to face me.

"My mom."

"She's a baker?"

"Well, after her and my dad split, she had to find a job. A bakery hired her for behind the counter help, but as the time went on, they needed more help in the kitchen and the woman trained her. You know what it's like in one parent households—the kids end up at their parent's work a lot." I smile and he nods, a quick look of guilt shadowing his features. "I picked up on things. There were times I'd help her out. I loved it but never thought of actually doing it for a living. And here I am."

"I can't thank you enough for stepping into the family business. My stomach thanks you, too." His grin spreads across his face and the space between my legs heats.

"So..." In an attempt to distract myself from my thoughts I grab a notepad and pen from the table behind me. "How many would you like me to make you each night? Or would you rather just do weekends? Or we could try it out and if it doesn't work..."

His hand warms my forearm.

"Relax." He dips his head to look me in the eyes.

They're searching mine and although I try to push back all of my desire for him, his chest rises and falls with a heavy breath showing me that I failed.

"Sorry. I'm just nervous for some reason." I drop the pen and clench my fists.

"Hey, it's me, Dane Murray, your friend."

I shake my head and stand up, getting as far away as I can, which lands me on the other side of the counter, my hands planted in front of me on the stainless steel.

"Don't," I warn and he holds his hands up in the air.

"Don't what?"

"Make a joke of the friend agreement."

He chuckles. "It's funny, you know." He looks up at the ceiling, his biceps on prominent display with his arms crossed over his chest. "Your cupcake tray kind of explains why people struggle with monogamy."

I scrunch my eyebrows, waiting for him to explain himself.

"Would you want only one flavor of cupcake for your entire life?"

"Yes, I would. I would be happy to eat a chocolate cupcake with coconut shavings everyday of my life." My tone is indignant. I'm not going to fall for his lure to get me to sleep with him again.

"Hey." He raises his hands in the air in defense. "I'm not saying anything, I'm just saying what if you marry some dude who can't give you chocolate one night, red velvet the next, and still be able to make your toes curl with vanilla?"

He stares at me, as though his point is proven.

"Why would I marry that person?" I round the prep station, needing something to do other than stare into those moss green eyes.

"You tell me." He gulps down more of his water and his Adam's apple bounces up and down. I can't help the desire that wells up inside. I want to run my tongue over the top of it and drag it all the way up to his ear.

Ugh. Back to the point at hand.

"Is this all because I said I couldn't have casual sex with you?"

"I don't think our sex would be casual. Applaudable, earth-shattering...those are better words for our sex."

I bite down on my lip, attempting to shelter the smile, but my cheeks are rising.

"Don't we think highly of ourselves? Earth-shattering?"

"Hey." His shoulders rise and fall. "I'm not giving all the credit to myself. You're a yoga master in some of the positions you contort yourself into."

Now I'm not only smiling like a goon, I'm blushing.

"Good to know I won't be some plain vanilla cupcake for the man I marry."

"Definitely not."

I nod thinking it's time put this topic to bed now.

"Where are you going with this conversation?" I ask.

"Just food for thought. I'm not built for one flavor the rest of my life. I like variety, but lately, I've been thinking, maybe variety doesn't have to mean numerous girls."

I cross my arms over my chest. "Did you have this epiphany before or after I shot you down?"

He puckers his lips. "Did you really shoot me down? I don't remember asking."

I almost reach for a cupcake to throw in his cocky, arrogant face, but the last thing I need is to smear frosting on an already edible body. I fear I'll end up licking it off.

"Answer the question," I grit out.

"Yeah." The stool slides across the floor when he stands. "See, after you this summer, I beat off to the image of you. My cock likes the memory of you bent over my desk, not to mention the memory of you straddling my face."

I blush and back away as he rounds the prep table.

"No one has really piqued my interest. I haven't really dated, and definitely haven't slept with anyone else. Then it dawned on me."

"It dawned on you. When you were fisting your cock to the image of fucking me?" That front I'm so used to putting on is crumbling as he approaches. I back up another step, trying to act indifferent to his stalking toward me.

He chuckles. "We've only been friends a few days and you already know me so well." He winks and my stomach disobeys my brain by flipping and flopping over and over again.

"I can be exclusive with you."

"I feel honored. Is this your way of asking me out?" I swallow the extra saliva building in my mouth. Damn, his shirt is so tight around those strong shoulders.

"I have a deal that I think we'll both be happy about."

"Which is?"

He stops a foot away from me, his thumb rubbing up and down the prep table. His gaze detours from mine as though he has to gather up the strength to say what he wants to. When he looks up, his eyes are swimming in determination.

"We can be exclusive friends with benefits." He holds up his two fingers in the air. "I promise I won't date or fuck anyone else while we're messing around."

"Scouts honor?" I give his two raised fingers a questioning gaze, knowing if Dane was ever a boy scout, it was solely to build fires and use a knife. "Why not a pinky promise?"

He tucks the two fingers into his fist and then he's holding his hand out to me with his pinky finger extended. His very large hand with those slim fingers that know exactly how to curl inside me and make me crazy.

I push my thighs together, clenching to push that memory away.

"I'm cool with a pinky promise."

I shake my head, spinning on the balls of my feet and walking to the fridge. Grabbing the bottle of vodka from the freezer, I twist it open and swallow down a shot.

Dane meets me there, grabbing the bottle from my

hands and pouring it down his own throat and then sets it on the counter.

"What do you say?" he asks, his gaze intent.

His deal is tempting. I can't deny the fact he rocked my world those two nights. The man is insatiable and I loved every second his hands, mouth and dick were all over and in me.

"No rules. No obligations. If anyone decides they meet someone they want to date then it's over?" I ask.

He nods, closing in on my space now. The promise that he'll rock my world is all over his face.

"No one can know about it. This is between us, after hours or secret places."

He nods, his finger skimming down my arm.

"No guy talk at the gym or in those single dad meetings."

He nods, stepping so close our bodies are flush together. God, he smells edible.

"Why?" I ask, wondering why he's willing to veer from his usual M.O.

His hand moves up until he's cupping my face, his thumb rubbing along my cheek. "I need to work you out of my system."

There it is. No romantic line about how much he needs me in my life. He wants to use me and move on. I'd harness the energy to be offended, but I think I need the same—get my fill of him—literally—and then move on to a normal, healthy relationship with someone who isn't such a commit-ment-phobe.

"Okay." I press my cheek into his palm and he bends his head down. "Pinky promise?" I ask again.

"Pinky promise," he whispers before sealing our deal with a kiss that weakens my knees, but I don't have to worry about falling because Dane's arm swings around my waist and hoists me up and swings me back around onto the prep table.

Is Dane the devil or a saint?

Neither. He's a fucking genius, especially with how he's mastered the way he uses his tongue.

11

AVA

The cool metal permeates through the thin fabric of my shirt while the heat of his body on top of me warms my front. I forgot how much I love the weight of him on me. How secure I feel with him.

The first two times we were together, our movements were frantic and uncontrolled, but tonight his hands move under the hem of my shirt, slower and more deliberate. Maybe he's been imagining doing this in his beat off sessions.

His large palm cups my breast and I wiggle under him, the ache in my pussy building.

"You have no idea how long I've wanted to feel your skin again." His mouth casts open kisses up my neck while his other hand reaches down and fiddles with the button of my jeans. "I can't wait to see what you're hiding under here."

The lightbulb goes off. Fuck.

I sit up and he slides off me. "What?" His eyes peer through the opening to the front door. "Did you hear something?"

"No. Um, I'm all for this." I motion with my finger between us. "Just not tonight."

I slide my breast into my white cotton bra and straighten my t-shirt.

Placing his hand on my hip, he maneuvers me to the edge of the table, pinning both arms on either side of me.

"Talk," he says, bending his head down once again, kissing my collarbone and my neck.

"Maybe we should think it over some more," I rush out.

"Do you not want me? Whenever and wherever you want?" His voice has that low timber that makes my core clench.

"Yes. I want you, but..." My thoughts trail off when he moves to the hollow of my neck, his tongue swirling until he reaches the other side.

"What is it Ava?" he murmurs against my heated skin.

My head lulls back and he takes the opportunity as an invitation.

"My tongue is magic, remember how good it felt working your pussy?"

His hand skims along the side of my stomach and his finger grazes along my stomach until his thumb and forefinger are flicking the button of my jeans again.

"Nope." I take two hands and push him off.

His eyes are wide with surprise but he's still staring at me like I'm his own batch of chocolate peanut butter cupcakes and he doesn't plan on leaving any crumbs behind.

"Okay." He holds his hands up. "I'm not gonna beg." He rounds the counter, swiping his phone and keys off the counter. "Let me know when you want to initiate our agreement."

Watching his back as he leaves feels like a jagged knife twisting in my stomach.

"Dane!" I call out.

He turns on his heels, leaning in the doorway in his usual suave, confident way. Somehow his position always seems to have the same affect on me as watching Magic Mike.

"What if we turn off the lights?" I ask.

Surely, that will be okay. There's no way I'm going to let him see me in my white cotton bra I'm wearing because it's my most comfortable and a pair of cotton panties that are jacked up to my naval because I haven't had time to laundry in three weeks. Said panties may or may not also have a tear around the elastic waistband.

"Nah, I'll wait. I need to see your body." He pushes off the doorframe and stands straight. "Why so shy?" His stance widens and he fiddles with the keys in his hands.

"Um..."

"I don't want to push you into anything, Ava. You have all the control."

I look down at the table. "It's just, I wasn't really prepared for this to happen tonight."

A deep chuckle floats out of him and he grabs his phone out of his back pocket and places it and his keys on the counter, stalking toward me.

"You need to shave?" he asks and my face heats to the level I imagine it would standing in front of an explosion. "Because that's okay."

"No, I shaved." Which must have been some sort of sixth sense because I hadn't since the rafting. "Um," I swallow. "Remember that pink see through matching bra and panty set you saw me in the first time?" He nods a deep breath causing his chest to rise and fall. "The second time, I had that sexy zip down athletic bra and nothing under my yoga pants."

"Best surprise." The corner of his lips upturns into a smile as he bites his bottom lip.

"Neither would be the case right now."

"So." He shrugs, and his hands grab the hem of my t-shirt, fiddling with it in his hands. "You were going to pass up on an earth-shattering sex marathon because you aren't wearing sexy lingerie?"

That sounds a tiny bit lame now that he says it out loud.

"Well..."

He pulls the t-shirt over my head, and my hands quickly wrap around my breasts to cover the bra.

Grabbing my forearms, he pries them apart and licks his lips. He reaches back, unhooking the clasp and it drops to the floor.

"One problem solved." He bends down, and his mouth takes my nipple into his mouth. His eyes glance up to mine, and my nipple pops out of his wet and inviting mouth. "I did like the bow though."

I roll my eyes and my breathing hiccups when his hands again move to the button of my pants. He slides them down my legs, his mouth sucking and licking my breasts the entire time. I wait for him to glance down. To look at what I'm wearing, but his fingers blindly pull both sides down my legs and he waits for me to step out of them before he flings them somewhere behind him.

Now that I'm standing in front of him naked, he kisses his way back up to my mouth.

"Better?" he softly asks against my lips.

"Better."

"Can I fuck you now?"

"You better." My hand reaches behind his head and pulls

it toward me. His tongue dives into my waiting mouth with determination.

Locking his head to mine, our lips and tongue search for a pace but nothing seems to quench the need in either of us. His hands search my body like it's the last time he can touch a woman and quickly, his fingers dig into my hips and he hoists me up onto the table.

Because he's so tall, we're even in height now and I strip him of his t-shirt, tossing it on the floor. My hands explore all the grooves and indents of his muscled chest.

"You're so fucking hot," I say and his lips close to smile against my lips. "I want to taste you," I whisper as his lips hover over mine.

"I could say the same." A smirk crosses his lips.

My hand explores, coming upon his pants and I flick the button open and slide the zipper down, his already hard cock pops out of the hole in the front of his boxer briefs, begging to be played with.

I squirm to get off the table, ready to take him in my mouth, but he stops me, his hand pressing on my chest until I'm lying flat.

"You'll have plenty of chances, but you've made me wait too long to taste you again."

He widens my legs, his head dipping between my thighs.

My body almost convulses when his tongue touches my clit. I arch my back, but he places his hand on the small of my stomach, keeping me down.

His tongue continues to manipulate my center, twirling and swirling, eating me like I'm his own personal cupcake made just for him, but when his teeth scrape along my clit, my entire body quivers for the orgasm he's spurring.

His finger pushes into me and then another one, filling me up.

"Dane!" I scream, my fist pounding the metal, needing something to grab onto.

Once he arches those strong fingers right to my G-spot I come like a freight train unable to stop. There's no yellow warning, my orgasm barrels through me straight from red to green.

His tongue slows, placing sweet kisses to my now trembling pussy until he's staring up at me. Propping up on my elbows, our eyes lock, and his hands reach for my hands, urging me up.

"Taste yourself," he says, his mouth covering mine. He pulls away. "See how addicting you are?"

I don't answer, not that I think he's expecting one. Using my heels, I push his jeans down to the floor and he toes out of his shoes and pushes everything off to the side, leaving him in a red pair of boxer briefs.

"I like it." I examine his rock-hard dick tenting the front of his boxer briefs.

"You're going to like it even more when it's deep inside you."

"I was talking about the boxers, but that too," I laugh, and he slides me to the edge of the table again.

Reaching down he fishes a condom out of the pocket of his jeans, tearing open the packet.

"Would you like me to do the honors?" I ask, sliding down from the table.

My feet land on the floor, but I fall to my knees, hooking both my fingers into his boxers and freeing the cock my mouth waters for.

He has such a beautiful cock. I swear before Dane, I never even knew you could attribute that word to a penis.

He hands me the condom. A small gasp escapes him when I roll it down and I know I don't have long before he hauls me onto the table to screw me. My body aches to feel him inside me.

His hand grabs my hips, and I'm sitting on the edge before I can blink. The one thing I realized when I've been with Dane in the past is that he has no qualms of placing me exactly where he wants me. There's something animalistic about it though, and that only excites me more.

I look into his eyes as he's guiding himself into me, there's so much lust and arousal in the room that it feels almost stifling. Inch by inch he pushes into me until he's as deep as he'll get. He moves one of my stray hairs from my ponytail behind my ear and leans in for a kiss.

Our kiss reaches the frantic stage fast, and he starts drilling into me repeatedly, his hands holding my legs up under my thighs as I'm hanging over the metal table. A table I'll be disinfecting tomorrow numerous times.

"Jesus, you always feel so fucking good," he says in my ear as he drags his cock in and out of me, his hips roll over and over again.

My ass rocks into him, our two bodies grinding together as moans and sighs bounce off every wall in the room. I place my palms flat against the metal, needing leverage to get him even deeper. My tits bounce up and down with each thrust, something he doesn't miss. His callused hands skim up my thighs to my hips and ass, continuing to dictate the rate we're going.

"I'll never get tired of you. I need this pussy every time I wake up. Be prepared for morning calls."

I have no doubt he's telling the truth.

"Harder, Dane. Harder," I pant, sweat starting to drip between my breasts.

His fingers grip my ass harder and he plunges into me with such ferocity, I gasp for a breath.

"Hard enough baby?" He continues to fuck me to the hilt and my arms are starting to lose strength, my legs already straining to hold up my weight.

"Yes."

He moves one leg to rest against his shoulder, hitting me in a completely different place inside. I gasp at the sheer amount of pleasure that rips through me every time he thrusts.

His thumb massages my clit and I feel my orgasm building. He continues working my body, his own sweat dripping onto my stomach.

"Damn, baby, your pussy is so fucking wet."

My hands find the edge of the table and I grip it hard to keep my body stable so he can hit that spot every time.

He skips a few gears and suddenly we're speeding up a hill and just like minutes earlier, there's no breaking, no warning, we fly right over the edge and I cry out.

My back arches off the now slippery surface and Dane's arm wraps around my leg in the air to make sure he continues to control my climax.

"That's it, baby, scream my name."

"Oh fuck, Dane!" I scream.

"Again." His face contorts into a half painful, half lust filled expression and he pumps into me one more time and stills.

"Ava," his voice is low and he twitches as he comes.

Done and spent, my arms extend out on the table and I catch the breath Dane stole from me.

This friends-with-benefits thing might just be the best decision I've ever made.

"Next time, we're using frosting." He winks, draws out of me and walks back to the bathroom.

I sit up, feeling slightly self-conscious now that it's all

over. He returns a second later as I'm throwing my t-shirt over my head.

"Name your flavor," I say, and he approaches me, swinging both arms around me.

"You know my favorite."

"Peanut butter and chocolate." I smile.

"Well, you actually, but I'll take what I can get." He winks and then takes the hem of my shirt and strips it from my body. "I'm not a one and done kind of guy. Let's eat some cupcakes and then fuck again."

"I'm not sure what you want more of...me or my cupcakes."

He swipes one from the tray and bites into it. "That's the beauty, I don't have to choose." He smirks, and I take my finger and dip it into the frosting of his cupcake. "There. Now, wipe that on your tit and I have my perfect dessert."

His words shouldn't ignite firecrackers inside my stomach, but damn if my body ever listens when it comes to Dane Murray.

12

DANE

I open the door to the Mad Batter and Toby and all his teammates file in along with their parents.

Ava's eyes widen as she places another tray of cookies in the glass case.

"What's going on?" she asks.

Toby runs up to the counter, his friends following closely behind. They huddle around Ava like she's Bryce Harper or some other Gatorade promoting player in the majors.

"Miss Ava, we won!" Toby screams and all the players start screaming.

They're all amped up after winning their first game of fall ball. Let's just say it's been a rough one.

"You did? Well, then, you need a cookie!" She pulls out a tray of her famous Eat Me cookies iced in pink and purple and turquoise.

The boys' hands freeze, none of them grabbing one.

"Those are for girls," one of them says.

Ava looks down and then places the tray back, pulling out another one with dinosaurs and teddy bears.

"Those are for babies," the same boy says, which stops every other boy from taking their fill.

"I swear, when I was young a cookie was a cookie." She looks over the heads of the boys to me, a smile in place. A smile I didn't used to get until our deal to be friends-with-benefits.

If I were arrogant I'd say she's smiling because she's still in the euphoria my dick created for her last night. But then I'd have to admit, I brought the boys here as an excuse to see her because I'm still in a state of bliss after last night, too.

"Sorry boys, that's all the kinds I have. I'll put it on my list to make some baseball ones, okay?"

All the boys shrug, and their hands dig in to grab one, appeased by her answer.

"Take a seat at the tables." I point to the section of tables one of the moms is pushing together.

They scramble and I wait for the parents to each place their order and find a seat in the small bakery. When it's finally my turn, I pull out my wallet to pay for the cookies.

"What would the coach like?" Ava bites down on her lower lip.

I lean over the counter. "Ten minutes with the baker in the storage room."

Ava pretends to look at the chalkboard sign above her head.

"Hmm, I don't see that." The spark in her hazel eyes is apparent and the caveman inside of me hopes her playfulness is due to last night.

"I think it's a special. Maybe exclusive for one person."

She giggles, grabbing a plate and placing a cookie on it, sliding it across the counter.

I glance down to the Eat Me cookie. "Are you giving me instructions now?" I look over my shoulder, finding the parents and kids busy and not paying us any attention. I pick it up and spread my tongue over the top in an exaggerated lick, flattening and widening it.

"You are truly something." She waves my antic off.

"You're the one who asked. I'm just displaying my skills." I bite the cookie, sliding the cash across the counter.

"Oh, I'm acquainted with your skills, Dane." Her own gaze takes in the room and then she slides the money back over to me.

"Cookies are on me."

"No, you don't." I slide it back her way. "Take it, really."

She hems and haws before, opening the cash register and grabbing my change.

"Thank you." She hands me the change, which I drop in the tip jar.

I look through the open window into the kitchen spotting a six-tier wedding cake on the table.

"Do you have a wedding or is that another one for the portfolio?"

She looks over her shoulder, dismissing it right away. "Portfolio."

"It's beautiful."

Just then one of the moms approaches the counter to grab some napkins and she checks out where we're looking.

"Did you make that?" she asks Ava.

Ava's face blushes and she nods, nibbling on the inside of her cheek.

"Yeah, she's a fantastic baker."

Ava shoots me a glare that says *shut-up.*

"Those flowers look so real. Are they?" the woman asks, craning her neck to see it.

"They're sugar." Ava steps to the side. "Would you like to see it?"

The mom, Krystal, eyes me, clearly surprised we have this kind of talent in Climax Cove, and then circles around the counter right through to the back. Ava and I follow.

"You should enter one of those cake competitions on the Food Network," Krystal says, walking around the cake like she's a judge. "Why the hell are you in Climax Cove?"

"Excuse me?" Ava asks.

"I mean, you're way too talented to be here. You should be in the city where people will spend five grand on a wedding cake." She focuses on the tray of sugar flowers that Ava must have been working on before the team barged in.

"Heidi, Kate, get in here and see this!" she calls out to the seating area.

Krystal, Heidi and Kate are like the mom brigade of Climax Cove. They have their hands in everything from fundraisers to extracurricular activities. They're the team moms, the PTA leaders, the volunteers at school. The overzealous, and overbearing kind of parents.

The tall blonde and the shorter brunette walk in, coffees in hand.

"Who did this?" Heidi swings her long blonde hair off her shoulders, stepping closer.

"She did." Krystal points to Ava who's about as red as a tomato and ready to hide under the table.

Heidi and Kate's eyes shift to Ava, both of their mouths ajar.

"It's gorgeous and makes me want to get married all over again," Kate says, setting her coffee down on the table.

"Thank you," Ava says with the smallest voice I've ever heard come out of her mouth.

"Whose is it?" Heidi asks.

"No one's. I just shoot it for my portfolio," Ava admits, and they all scoff.

"What do you do with the cake?" Kate asks.

"The last one I made, I took down to Veteran's Hall."

They all nod, their eyes focused on the extravagant cake.

"Oh my God! I have the best idea," Kate says, pulling her phone out of her jacket.

Ava's eyes shift to mine in a *what's going on* question.

Kate walks away toward the storage room, whispering into the phone and by the time she returns she's smiling so wide you'd think someone just told her she doesn't have to do any more school fundraisers for the rest of her life.

"So, I'm hoping it's okay, but I have my in-laws walking down here."

I smile knowing exactly what Kate just did.

Based on Ava's fidgeting with her hands she's skeptical. "Okay. Why?"

The boys are getting louder and I know most of the dads are probably just talking sports and not paying attention and the last thing I want is for the boys to break something in her shop. So, I walk over to the window and take a peek, finding them all flipping a water bottle in the air to see how it lands.

"Boys, simmer down."

One of the dads catches me and waves me off to say he'll handle it.

"I'm married to Donnie Vitner, his parents own Double D's," Kate says.

"Okay. And?" Ava asks, her gaze shifting to me.

"They could take the cake off your hands once you're finished with it and serve it at the restaurant. At least you'd get something for it."

"Not the five grand like she should." Krystal is still in awe. "If I ever get a ring on this finger again," she holds up her hands, wiggling her ring finger, "you're doing my cake."

I could make a few jokes right now, but I'm not about to ruin this for Ava.

"Katie?" Debbie's voice hollers into the bakery.

"Back here, Ma," Kate says and a second later Debbie walks in and her jaw hits the floor.

"You weren't lying." Debbie takes her time to examine the cake as though it won't be sliced into pieces and served.

"Hi, Ava, sorry I haven't been by yet," Debbie says.

"So, Ava," Kate interrupts. "The diner used to get pies from the Baking Basket before Norma closed. Lately, my father-in-law has been trying to bake the desserts himself." She shares a look with Debbie. "It's not working out very well," Kate adds.

"He's more of a BLT and burger type cook." Debbie pats Ava's arm.

"I don't know why we didn't think about this sooner," Kate says, shaking her head.

"Then it's set." Ava's gaze shifts to me when I finally speak after hanging out in the background.

"How much?" Debbie asks. "I'll definitely take the cakes after you're finished with them. How many are you planning on doing?"

"Um." Ava hiccups for a response, probably not used to how fast things can get done in a small town. No emails, texts or voice messages. All business is done face-to-face.

"She'll make one a week. You can freeze the layers and take them out as needed. You'll pay half of what she'd normally charge?" I quirk my eyebrow to Ava to make sure it sounds fair.

She nods. "Or I could make you other cakes?" she offers.

I shake my head. She's too much of a people pleaser. Not that I'm upset when she's pleasuring me.

Luckily Debbie beats me to it.

"No, this is perfect and we don't have any waste. Plus, Don will look at it like he's getting a deal." Her and Kate laugh.

Don Senior is known for stretching his pennies.

"Okay, thank you. I'm almost finished and then I can snap a few pictures and get it down to you."

Debbie smiles. "Perfect. By dinner tonight?"

"Yes. That sounds good." Ava's smile gleams.

"Looking forward to our business partnership. Oh, and I was at Dane's grill the other day and had one of your strawberry margarita cupcakes. Oh my, that was delicious. Worth every gripe from Don about spending so much on flour and sugar." She smiles and Kate laughs.

"Thank you." Ava holds out her hand to Debbie who stares down at it and then to me.

I shrug in a what-can-I-say-she's-not-a-native-in-Climax-Cove.

"I seal my deals with a hug." Debbie steps closer, wrapping her arms around Ava, who at first seems hesitant but eventually reciprocates.

A crash comes from the front room and I don't hear any of the boy's voices anymore. All of us run to the doorway to find the boys circled around a teapot pointing fingers to one another in a *he did it* echo.

"Boys," I say and all their scared faces look at me. "Who did it?" I walk into the room and they continue to point and blame one another.

My eyes focus on Toby, but Ava comes to my side with a broom and dustpan.

"It's okay," she says, starting to use the broom to sweep it up.

"Toby?" I question and when his matching green eyes meet mine I shift my eyes to Ava.

"I'll do that Miss Ava." He holds his hands out to Ava.

Then another boy grabs the dustpan.

"Thank you boys, that's very polite of you." Ava steps back, running right into my back.

I place my hands on her shoulders and lean down to whisper. "I'll pay to replace it."

She circles around and my eyes can't stop staring at her lips, remembering them on my skin last night.

"Not necessary." She slides away and goes behind the counter.

As my eyes track her, I catch Krystal, Heidi and Kate all staring over at me with smirks that suggest they're running scenarios in their heads. I'm sure it'll be all over the circuit soon that the town bar owner and bakery owner are hitting homeruns in the back room.

Once the mess is cleaned up, we say our goodbyes and I get the boys out of the bakery before something else breaks. Heidi has taken Toby with her since he has plans to sleep-over at her place for her son's birthday so I have the rest of the day to myself.

No sooner have I sat down in the chair in my office, when my phone chimes.

AVA: DO YOU THINK THAT DEAL IS FAIR?

Me: Definitely.

Ava: Thanks for negotiating. I was just surprised.

Me: I look forward to collecting my commission.

Ava: Commission?

Me: My cut for closing the deal.

Ava: Do I even want to know what you want?

Me: Oh, believe me you do. ;)

Ava: Does it involve me on my knees?

Me: I would never ask you to do something you don't want to do.

Ava: Don't make assumptions.

Me: How about a striptease?

Ava: Oh, you can do better than that ...

Me: Tonight. My place. Toby's at a sleepover for a birthday party.

Ava: Time?

Me: Seven.

Ava: I'll bring the kneepads.

I CHUCKLE, MY THUMBS ALREADY MOVING.

ME: I COULD GET USED TO THIS FRIENDS-WITH-BENEFITS thing.

SHE NEVER ANSWERS AND MY GAZE FINDS THE CLOCK, SEEING I still have six hours before my mouth is on hers. I lean back in my chair contemplating the fact that it's the first time I can remember ever counting down the hours until I got to see a woman.

13

DANE

I glance at the clock when I finally walk into my house. Six fifty.

I search the room, deciphering where to start.

Toby and I built a fort Thursday and watched Goonies. The blankets are still strewn everywhere and covering the couch I plan to use to watch a movie with Ava later.

Moving my gaze to the kitchen, I see breakfast from this morning in the sink.

So, I'm not much of a cleaner. Ava has to already assume that about me.

Scrambling I figure the kitchen being clean is more important than a few blankets that need folding.

I turn on the water, getting the sink cleaned out and loading the dishwasher. Glancing at the kitchen table, I sigh and my head falls back.

Toby's iPad, baseball cards, and a bunch of other crap is everywhere along with dried cereal from this morning. Instead of picking each item up, I grab the laundry basket that was for the clothes in the dryer and swipe my arm along the entire surface, effectively cleaning off the table.

Now we have somewhere to eat.

On the way to Toby's room, I pick up all his stuff that you'd think must just fall out of his pockets as he walks around and drop the basket into his room, closing the door behind me.

The place is halfway decent now and my feet are moving to the family room to tear down the fort when the doorbell rings.

Should I have expected anything less than for Ava to be on time?

She's smiling and eyeing me when I open the door.

Is she remembering the first time she was here because I wouldn't mind her stripping in my foyer again.

"Hey," she says, both her hands clutching her purse in front of her.

"Come in." I step aside and open the door wider.

She peruses the area, her first time here with the lights on.

"Thank you." Her heels click on my wooden floors and it's the first time I've ever seen her in anything but Chucks.

"So, I'm going to be honest with you. I'm not an Alice." I grab Toby's cup off the counter and stuff it in a drawer.

"Alice?" she asks, still looking around.

"You know from the Brady Bunch. Alice the housekeeper."

She nods. "Oh. It's okay, I didn't think you would be."

"Stereotyping me?" I ask her, grabbing her purse and placing it on the table. "Relax."

She nods a few times, her eyes on the purse I just laid down. "Is it stereotyping when you find out it's the truth?"

I chuckle, grabbing her hand and leading her through the house to the back door.

"I suppose not." I open the screen door and wait for her to walk out first.

The minute the light salty air hits us, she smiles and inhales a deep breath.

"Talk about beautiful." She takes no time to slip off her heels and wiggle her toes in the sand that bumps up to the edge of the deck.

I wait a second, admiring her ass in a pair of jeans rolled at the ankles and a blouse that falls over her left shoulder, exposing the sun-kissed skin I love to kiss. Usually she's a jeans and t-shirt kind of girl.

She's still wearing jeans and you always see her at the bakery. What do you expect her to wear, a ball gown and diamonds?

Her head swivels both ways, finding us secluded except for my parent's house farther back off the beach, but close enough to see that their lights are on.

"It's peaceful." She looks over her shoulder, smiling.

"That's what I love the most about it." I meet her at the end of the deck, not stepping in the sand since I'm wearing my boots.

"You?" she asks with a laugh about to rise up her throat.

"Yes, me. Why do you say that?"

"You like to be the center of attention, life of the party, take nothing seriously." She sits down on the edge of my deck.

"Do you want a drink?" I ask.

"Sure."

I run inside, grab two beers and return to the deck after disposing of my boots and socks.

"Here." I twist the cap off and hand her over a bottle.

"What were we talking about?" I sit down next to her.

She's wearing perfume tonight. Perfume that makes me want to push her onto her back and have my way with her.

"How you take nothing seriously." She raises her eyebrows.

"I just like to have fun in life. That's all."

She nods. "I think you want people to believe that."

We lock eyes for a moment, but she turns away. "Sorry, I shouldn't do that. I'm always telling people what I see and that's not what this is about." Her eyes roam over my body.

"What this is about?"

She stands. "Friends with benefits. Nothing serious, right?" She startles me and I set my beer down on the deck to have two free hands.

"Well, friends find things out about each other." My hands squeeze her ass.

"I'd rather get to the benefits." Her fingers unbutton her top button on her blouse and she starts working her way down. "There's no white cotton bra tonight."

"No?" My eyes fixate on her fingers, her painted fingernails.

"I opted for something a tad sexier." She opens her blouse and she's wearing a black see-through bra with a red satin fabric spread across her bare breasts and tied into a bow.

"A present for me? It's not even my birthday." I flex my hands, exaggerating the movement in preparation to get my hands on her.

Her head falls back in laughter, and she steps a little closer to me.

"Go ahead." She leans forward, her breath tickling my ear. "Open me."

I look around like someone would have appeared in the

two seconds she straddled my lap and stripped open her blouse.

My fingers grab each end of the bow and I pull. The fabric falls to her sides and there are those pink nipples peaked and ready to be played with.

"Damn, you're sexy as hell."

My one arm swings around her and I pull her closer to me so I can place my mouth over her breast.

Her fingers run along my neck, and one arm raises up until she's pulling on my strands, keeping me right where she wants me.

"I think it's safe to say you like your present?" She giggles.

"Uh huh," I mumble into her breast, my tongue licking and swirling around her pebbled nipple.

She slides back, and her breast pops out of my mouth. "What are you doing?" I reach out to grab her again, but she shakes her head.

She stands up and unbuttons her jeans before kneeling on the bottom of the deck stoop.

"I think it's time for gift number two."

Pulling the hem of my shirt up she unfastens my jeans and pushes me to lean back so she can unzip my pants.

"Hey, I was good with where we were going."

"Why are you always so quick not to let me suck you off?" She falls back on her heels. Her tits are right there and waiting for my hands.

"I never want you to think you have to do anything like that," I say honestly.

"Dane." She rises, leaning over to me so our lips are almost touching. "I want to taste you. I want to feel you crumble in ecstasy while you shoot your load into my mouth. And I really want to swallow you down my throat."

"Fuck. Your dirty words almost finished the job before your mouth did."

I've never been with a girl who talked as dirty as I did and now I see that I've been missing out. This woman is phenomenal.

She giggles and grabs the waist of my jeans and boxers, shimmying them down my legs with help from me.

Her hand fists me first, running up and down along my cock in a swirling motion. I wish we were on my couch so I could lean back and relax, but then I'd probably close my eyes and miss the first time those pretty plump lips cover my dick. Her pale pink glossed lips open and she takes me into her mouth.

It isn't the tip of my dick hitting the back of her throat or her hand pumping the bottom of my shaft that makes me grow harder. It's the inaudible moan that rises and floats out of her mouth and into the dusky night air above us.

"Holy shit." My hand moves to her hair, fisting her dark strands around my hand, keeping her right there. Doing exactly what she's doing.

Her free hand skates along my inner thigh until she cups my balls, playing with them in her hand.

A groan escapes as she sucks her cheeks in while she draws her mouth up my straining length and swirls her tongue around the head. Without pausing, she pushes back down on my cock until I reach the back of her throat. She does this over and over again until I can barely keep my head up and my eyes open to watch what is absolutely going to be the number one feature on my rub reel from now on.

My orgasm is right there, begging for the torture to end, but I'm promising myself it will be so much more intense if I can hold off a little longer.

"I don't wanna know where you learned to suck cock like this or focus on the fact that you own that bra."

Her soft giggle is still audible over her slurping as her saliva covers my cock and drips down over my balls.

She continues to moan and groan while the ocean waves make land, and I'm trying to not come, but then she does some sort of twisting action with her hands and mouth at the same time and all my stomach muscles contract as I jolt up, gripping her hair tighter.

"Oh, shit."

I come down her throat and she stays there until my cock stops twitching, swallowing every drop of me.

By the time she rises, I see that at some point she's stuck her hand down her own pants and that's all my dick needs to go full salute again.

She licks her lips and then slides closer to me, bringing her lips to mine. "Want to taste yourself?" she asks, just like I did to her.

Then she giggles, standing up and grabbing my hand.

"Mind if we go inside now? I saw a fort I wouldn't mind being lost in for a few hours." She walks to the back door as I try to pull my pants and boxers up and keep pace.

She keeps the doorknob in her hand and her back pressed against the door.

I barricade her in, my lips millimeters from hers.

"Is it time for my benefits now?" she asks in a sultry voice that makes my balls tighten.

"Tell me what you want...rope, dildo, handcuffs?" I turn the knob and we fall into the house.

"How about all three?" she says and runs into the fort.

"A girl after my own heart."

14

Dane pulls up his pants, and I throw my t-shirt back on.

"Hurry. She's going to be here in like ten minutes," I say to Dane who I'm about to shove out the window like he's my high school boyfriend and my dad's knocking on the door.

"I am, but I'm not about to zip up my dick so Charlie doesn't find out about us." He slowly tucks himself in and then pulls the zipper up at a tortoise pace.

"Okay," I take my two hands and direct him to the door. "Now you go."

"I kind of like these afternoon quickies." He turns, and I circle him back around, my two hands on his back, forcing him down the hallway.

"Yeah, why is that?"

"Your mouth is dirtier during the daylight hours." He chuckles and walks down the stairs just as the doorbell rings.

"I could say the same about you."

We reach the bottom and he circles around again,

picking me up. "I really do love your pussy just so you know. And your taste. I'm not lying when I say those things. It's not a heat of the moment kinda thing."

I laugh because when it comes to Dane I can't not. "Well, thank you. I'm glad you find my pussy flavorful."

He kisses me short and sweet and then my feet land on the floor. I swing open the door, finding a package on the stoop. I pick it up and feel my face heat when I see where the box is from. Dane pounces like the good observer he is.

"What's in the package?" he asks.

"Nothing." I toss it on the table and walk past him to grab his jacket off the couch. "Something for Charlie."

It's wrapped in brown paper, so he'll have no idea. I turn at the same moment his eyes scan the package.

"Did Charlie change her name to Ava Pearson?" he asks, raising both eyebrows.

"It's nothing. Let it go."

He picks it up. "Are you keeping secrets from me? What is Your Hart's Desire Products?" He acts like a seven-year-old trying to figure out his Christmas present by shaking the package. "It's rectangular."

I snatch it out of his hands. "It's private." I hold it to my chest.

"Do I really not satisfy you?"

I crinkle my brow.

"I know what Your Hart's Desire Products are Ava. I don't live under a rock."

Of course he knows the sex toy company that Cat's sister's friend owns. Why wouldn't he?

"The owner comes up and stays at Garrett's cabin every year."

Well, I didn't know that, not that I care. I'm not going to

stalk her and ask for samples. But still, I should find out what the hype of this unicorn cock thing is anyway.

"Am I not pleasing you enough?" He seems really bothered by that notion.

I smack him with the package and he rubs his hand over it. "Let's not bruise the goods, okay?"

I laugh and he smirks.

The room grows quiet. "I'm serious though."

Walking to him, I jump in his arms. "You pleasure me just fine." *More than fine if I'm being honest.* "This is for our off nights. I bought one because Cat and Charlie were bragging about it and I wanted to know what it's all about."

He stares for an uncomfortable few seconds. "You're telling me that you've never used a dildo?"

I shake my head.

"Butt plug? Nipple clamps?"

I shake my head again.

"Anal beads? Ben Wa balls?"

"Okay, now I'm wondering what you haven't tried. No wonder you knew what Hart products were."

He smiles. "Variety is the spice of life, right?" He winks and continues. "The thought of using a dildo on you intrigues me. Can you show me?"

I wiggle out of his hold and stare down at the package. Glancing at the clock, I see we only have five minutes before Charlie should be home.

"Quick, okay?"

"Hey, we're dressed. I can say I stopped by to see her."

I rip open the package and pull out the Unicorn Cock I bought.

"Unicorn Cock?" he asks, grabbing it from my hands and turning it around and around in his hands. "This is bullshit."

"What?"

"It says that every girl should find their unicorn cock but in the meantime, enjoy this." He looks at me without an ounce of humor in his eyes. "I'm your Unicorn Cock."

I take it out of his hands. "Why would you say that?"

He approaches me. "Bring this to my office tonight and I'll show you who your unicorn cock is."

"Maybe." I bite my bottom lip. Is he...jealous? Of an inanimate object?

A key inserts in the door and my eyes widen, and my gaze scrambles around the tiny area, to do what, I have no idea.

"I told you!" I point my finger at him, but he turns around, his shoulders relaxed.

Opening the door for Charlie she stumbles in, her hand still on the key in the door. She looks up to see Dane and then looks behind him to me and then back to Dane.

"Hey, boss." She takes the key out of the lock and walks the rest of the way into the house.

"Hey, Charlie. Just finalizing my cupcake order for this week." He waves his hand up in the air. "Thanks, Ava, see you later." He shuts the door behind him leaving me alone with a very curious and skeptical Charlie.

"You're screwing Dane Murray?" Charlie asks, flipping through the envelopes of mail on the table.

"No!" My voice not even close to normal.

"Okay." Her tone suggesting I'm lying.

"I'm serious, Charlie."

She doesn't say a word and walks into the kitchen.

I follow.

"Charlie," I call out after her but she never turns around. "I'm not."

She pulls down a bowl from the cabinet and pours

cereal into it. "It's none of my business if you are, but I'll tell you this." She points her spoon my way. "If you somehow get together with Dane and Cat's with Marcus, I'm not going to be with Garrett."

I slide into a chair at the table. "I'd think you'd like that scenario."

She pours the milk and then digs her spoon into her Lucky Charms.

"Why would you say that?" she asks, not bothering to look my way.

"Charlie, most of the town knows you lust after Garrett Shaw."

She shakes her head. "He's one of those childhood crushes that's all. My big brother's best friend. He's too heartbroken to ever be serious with another woman. I doubt he's even the guy I crushed on anymore anyway."

"I bet he's in there somewhere. Maybe he needs you to dig him out."

Just then the back door swings open and Cat bursts through, panting for breath.

"What are you doing?" I ask.

She's never at the apartment anymore since she's usually at Marcus' place.

"I ran down here from Marcus'." She bends at the waist, heaving and trying to suck air into her lungs.

"Why?" Charlie asks in her usual laisse-faire manner.

"I'm having a hard time in the creativity department. I used to run in college when the same thing would happen in college, so I figured I'd try it out. Turns out I'm out of shape and I think I've gained twenty pounds since meeting Marcus."

She grabs a water from the fridge and sits down, loudly gulping down half the bottle.

"What's up with you guys?" she asks, still short of breath.

"Ava's screwing Dane."

"Charlie!" I screech but she only winks over the spoon of Lucky Charms going into her mouth.

"Really?" Cat looks at me, not nearly as surprised as she should be.

"You already knew?" I deadpan.

She shrugs.

"So, I was the only one left out in the cold?" Charlie questions, chomping down on her cereal.

"I assumed. Ava never confirmed," Cat clarifies and I want to slink down.

"Well, he was just over here and they were bumping uglies or whatever."

"Who's watching the bakery?" Cat asks.

"I closed it for an hour. I need to find some help though."

"You closed it so you could fuck Dane? Why not just use the storage room?" Charlie asks.

I shrug.

"We've done it there. We've done it in his office, on my prep table, his house. Hell, we even went on a hike and banged. Thank God, I didn't get poison ivy. In the last three weeks, I've screwed Dane everywhere imaginative and unique. I'm having a hard time keeping up with this foreign version of myself as a sex kitten."

Charlie rounds the counter and sits at the table.

"Are you guys dating?" Cat asks, finally able to talk normally now.

"No." I pick at the skin around my fingernails. "We're just friends with benefits."

Charlie lets loose a mocking laugh. "Yeah, okay."

"What?" I ask, confused by her reaction.

"Ava, how old are you? You know one of you will be hurt in the end and my money is on you," Charlie says.

I study the table, knowing she might be right. "It was going great until I felt like I always had to keep being exciting," I say.

"Why do you think that?" Cat leans forward.

I rub my hand on my face. "Because I told Dane I wouldn't do the friends-with-benefits if he was screwing around with other women."

"So, you guys agreed to a monogamous friends-with-benefits situation?" Charlie stifles a laugh that looks like it's begging to escape.

"Yeah," I shrug.

"You're both morons." The chair Charlie is sitting in slides along the floor as she gets up.

"Why do you say that?" I ask, a little hurt by her reaction.

Even Cat is biting the inside of her cheek. Was it really that stupid of a notion?

"Ava, think about it. You guys are dating. You only see each other," Charlie says.

"No, we only fuck each other," I clarify.

"Same difference if you ask me. Just because he doesn't pick you up, take you to a nice restaurant or buy you flowers, you think it's any different?" Charlie tosses her bowl in the sink and leans against the counter, staring me down. "I'm guessing you probably don't strip off your clothes, fuck, and then leave, right?" She quirks her eyebrow.

"Well." I try to fight it, but the truth is, we usually share a meal and oh God, some conversation about our day. The memory of laying in a fort as he told me how his whiskey distributor screwed him over and how he has some new guy coming up next week replays in my mind. Or when I told him how I burnt three batches of cupcakes and had to air out the shop for an hour.

"Sometimes yes, we focus on the friends part, but that doesn't mean anything."

Charlie pulls her unruly curly hair into a ponytail, her eyes digging into me like she's some detective waiting for me to crack under the pressure of her scrutiny.

My gaze shifts to Cat. Surely, she understands.

"I'm not looking for a relationship," I argue my position some more, my eyes meeting Charlie's head-on like a game of chicken.

"Isn't that when you fall into one?" Charlie's cocky smirk let's me know why she gets along with Dane so well. They're two peas in a pod.

I stand up, knocking over Cat's bottle and it spills all over the table.

"I don't need to justify my actions. We're having fun, with no strings, and yes it's monogamous but that means nothing." I stomp out of the room and then pause. "Sorry for spilling the water." Then I spin on my heel, grab my keys, and leave out the front door.

Charlie. Ha. Like I need to take advice from a girl who's pining away for a man who'll never allow himself to be available again. She has no idea what she's talking about. Our arrangement is working out wonderfully and I see no reason to let what she said get into my head.

This argument is working. I don't care about anything but Dane's dick.

And maybe his hands.

His mouth, too.

I don't care about anything but Dane's body.

There.

I turn the corner to get back to the bakery, but I step

back to hide behind the brick wall of the building on the corner as my heart drops to the pit of my stomach. Scratch that. It splatters to the concrete ground, cracking open and dying a slow death on the corner of Main and Maple while I watch Dane open the door of his Mustang for a brunette in a pair of Daisy Duke shorts and a tank top.

The smile on his face is as bright as the sun shining in the sky.

That asshole played me. He played me well.

"Thanks for coming." I pull my car away from the curb.

"I can't believe you still drive around in this car." Sara touches the hood and glances back to the backseat. "He rides in the back?"

I look at the empty cup from Double D's and his paper hat from the other night. "Yeah."

"Thanks for the pictures." She crosses her legs and while she's fidgeting, I try to give her the once over, not really sure what she's up to these days.

"Well, I figure a mother would want to know." There's a little more bite in my voice than I intended.

"Who'd figure a screw up like me could make such an attractive kid?"

She asks the question, but I know she's not looking for answers. Sara's never been a real mom, and she seemed to have sensed that after a short time. A year to be exact. Toby woke up on his first birthday without a mom to care for him.

We drive down the road and I could ask what's been going on in her life. Where she's been, who she's been with, does she have any money, how she got here. But the truth is, I had to leave Sara to her own demise years ago. I couldn't save her and that was just the hard truth.

"Happy Daze looks good. You've made a success out of it after all these years."

"Thank you. Yeah, had to fight tooth and nail for every change, but it was worth it."

"Do you ever wonder what it'd be like if I'd stayed? What your life would be like?" she asks the same question I thought of a lot early on in Toby's life. But only because of the insecurity that plagued me when I worried I couldn't be the father he deserved. Now, years later, I can't imagine my life any other way. Without Toby, it's nothing.

I shrug. "Doesn't everyone wonder about decisions in their life?"

"I look at other moms and I think to myself, why can't I be like them? What's wrong with me that I just can't stay in Climax Cove and take care of my kid? Or maybe I could've been one of those moms who drift around with their kid. I could have taken Toby with me."

"To sleazy motels and drug houses? Have him help you panhandle for food?" The bitterness in my tone can't be disguised as anything different.

The one unselfish thing Sara ever did was leave Toby behind. Let him have a normal childhood back in the same town she grew up in. Yeah, she was always the small-town girl who couldn't break out fast enough. I'm not sure when she transformed into that person. High school, junior high, or whether she was born like that, but I always remember her wanting out.

"When you put it that way..." she doesn't finish because we both know Sara can't care for herself let alone a child. "I'm afraid he'll hate me."

"I'll make sure he doesn't hate you, but I can't say he won't come looking when he gets older."

"You never came looking." There's a hint of sadness in her voice, but we both know the truth.

"You didn't want to be found."

She nods.

"You'll make sure he knows I love him?" Her voice cracks and I look down at her chipped nail polish and broken nails. A million cheap silver rings on her fingers and bracelets on her arm. What happened to the girl next door who won Miss Climax Cove?

"Of course."

I reach over and cover her hand with mine. "I promise, but Sara, you're making a good decision."

She nods and I slide one hand from under mine, swiping a tear from her eye.

I'm unsure whether to trust the tears. They've come in the form of manipulation so many times before.

I pull into my driveway, park, and run inside.

Grabbing the papers from my underwear drawer in my dresser so they've stayed hidden from Toby, I lock up and jog back out to my car.

I hand them to her and then pull out of the driveway and head back to downtown.

"It seems silly that this is all it takes to not have your kid be yours anymore." She flips through the pages with Post-It notes that indicate where to sign and date.

I ignore her comment because I'm not sure what she wants me to say.

By the time we're parked outside Happy Daze, it's growing close to when Toby gets out of school and the last thing I need is for them to see one another.

"Hold up, Sara." I hold my finger up and jog across the street to see if Ava would mind grabbing Toby after school.

The minute I open the door to Mad Batter, something is different. The energy is different, not the usual light and welcoming mood.

A pounding in the back tells me where to find her.

She's kneading and hammering a rolling pin on a ball of blue something.

"Hey."

She looks up, surprised to see me.

"Why do you think you can just come back here?" Her eyes are laser pointed at me and I feel like I should be covering my nuts before she takes a shot at them.

I take my life in my hands and erase the distance between us, coming up behind her. "You usually like it when I'm back here. Usually it's me pounding something on the table." I drop my tone an octave lower.

She swivels around, the rolling pin high in her hands. "Do you think I'm stupid? That you can just go off and I wouldn't find out? And let's not even talk about the part where your dick moved from me to her in a half hour time frame. You know what..." she raises the rolling pin higher and starts wiggling it, so I grab her wrist, pulling it back down until the rolling pin falls to the table.

"Enlighten me on what the hell you're talking about."

"Daisy Duke girl ring a bell?" She slides by me, mostly because I can't believe she saw Sara.

"It's nothing, okay?"

She opens the fridge, grabbing another pile of the same shit she was working on except this time it's pink, then picks up a rolling pin again.

"It's nothing," she mimics me. "You're so full of shit, Dane Murray. And I'm the naive girl who believed your lies.

Well," there goes the rolling pin back up in the air, "not this time around. This time it's over. O.V.E.R. Over."

She takes out all her aggression on whatever that stuff is on the table.

"Listen, give me an hour and I'll explain everything. I promise. But I can tell you for certain, I'm not screwing Sara."

"Sara. Oh, the whore has a name? Dane and Sara Murray what a ring that has to it."

I can't stop my laugh from escaping when she uses our names like that.

Her eyes narrow and if this were a cartoon like Toby watches, there'd be steam pouring out of her ears. "Get out, if you know what's good for you!" She stalks toward me, dropping the rolling pin on the table.

I grab both her hands and smash my lips to hers. She tries to fight me, her small little bunched up hands hitting my chest, but when I slide my tongue into her mouth, she loses the fight, kissing me back. That doesn't last long and she takes her two hands and pushes me off her.

"Don't distract me."

"Listen." I cage her between my arms, giving her no space to leave, praying she doesn't knee me in the groin. "I'll be back in one hour with an explanation. A very good explanation and you'll look back at this moment and laugh. But I need a favor."

She crosses her arms over her chest and raises a brow. "Go figure."

I smile, hoping to turn this around. "Can you grab Toby for me and bring him here?"

"You better not be asking me to watch your son while you go screw someone else or so help me God, Dane—"

"The only person I'm screwing right now is you." I kiss her forehead and feel her body soften against me.

"Are you making a fool of me?" she asks in a small voice.

"Never. I promise." I hold up my one hand with my pinky sticking out. "I pinky promise."

This earns me a smile.

"Okay, fine. One hour and I want an explanation the minute you walk through that door."

"You got it." I bend down and kiss her lips, wishing I could stay and fuck all that aggression out of her.

Nothing's better than angry sex.

"I'll be back," I say.

I run out of the shop and find Sara on the phone. She's crying to someone with the papers crumbled in her hands. Damn, I knew I was taking a chance leaving her alone without making sure this was headed in the right direction.

"Sara?"

"I gotta go." She hangs up the phone and shoots those brown puppy dog eyes she's used so expertly to get her way over the years in my direction.

"I'm not sure, Dane." She rummages through the papers, flipping one after the other. "It says I no longer have any rights."

Okay, stay calm and collected. Do not go off on her.

"Sara." I put my arm around her shoulders, looking up to the sky and praying Ava isn't watching out her window. Leading us toward Mike Polar's law office. "This is what's best for him. I'm assuming you've battled with this decision since I tracked you down?"

She nods.

I figured since it took her over a year to get back to me and agree to sign the adoption papers.

I open the door to the lawyer's office and then close it, detouring us to the side of the building.

"I'm not going to force you, Sara. This is your decision and if you're not ready then okay."

"What if I told you I want to take him with me?"

I thread my fingers through my hair. "Then I'd have to say I'll see you in court. I won't let Toby live that life, Sara and I think you know I have a better case than you."

She blows out a breath, staring at the papers in her hand.

"Will you continue to send me pictures?"

"Yes."

She nods a few times. "That was my boyfriend. He's waiting for me at the bus station in Wet Rock."

I raise my eyebrows, stuffing my hands in my pockets. I don't want to sway her either way. This has to be her decision.

"Okay, this is best for him. I know that." A tear runs down her cheek.

She opens the door herself and sits down in a chair while I walk up to Linda, the receptionist.

"Mike will be right with you," she says.

I sit down next to Sara and wrap my arm around her shoulders to pull her into me.

"I'm a horrible person," she mumbles into my chest.

I had suspicions that her double guessing was guilt and not necessarily want.

"You're not horrible." The words are hard to say because I never understood why Toby wasn't enough for Sara to stop what she thinks is a fun lifestyle.

Mike's office door opens and he eyes the scene in front of him, questioning me with his raised brows.

I nod, standing up but keeping Sara near me.

We file into the office and sit down across from Mike.

Mike hands a pen to me and to Sara. "Linda, I need you to witness."

She comes in the office. Linda used to be my Catholic religion education teacher. Sara's too actually. I wonder what she thinks about this situation.

She notarizes the papers and shuffles out of the office without a word, shutting the door behind her.

"So, I'll file these with the courts, but as the papers say, Dane is now the acting legal guardian." Mike looks at Sara.

"He's always been the responsible one," Sara mumbles.

Mike laughs but catches himself. "In this case, he is." He winks at me before standing up.

"That's it?" I ask.

"That's it. I'll be in touch with you as soon as everything comes back," he says to me then switches his attention back to Sara. "Good luck, Sara."

She wipes a few more tears and I eye the clock in his office. Fifteen minutes before Toby gets out of school.

"Let's go," I say.

I shuffle her out of the office and down the street while she tucks her head down, probably trying to not be recognized. Hell, I didn't tell anyone she was going to be in town. That was a stipulation I had to promise to before she agreed to come.

We get into my Mustang and I'm driving out of town to Wet Rock well before Toby would ever walk down Main Street.

"Thanks, Dane," she says when I park in a spot outside the bus station.

"The least I can do is give you a ride."

I spot a guy on a bench. He's got baggy jeans and a tight

t-shirt on. His hair stuck up in every direction. Looks like her usual type of loser.

"It's not that. Thanks for taking care of Toby." She reaches over pulling me in tight. "You sacrificed for me."

"I don't see it as a sacrifice, Sara. I'm sorry that you always did."

She pulls back, tears welling in her coffee-colored eyes.

"Why?" she asks, her voice shallow I almost missed the question. "Why did you take him in?"

I shrug. "It's simple. I love him."

"As your own?"

"I've never not thought of him as anything but my own."

She glances to the window, the loser now standing up, noticing it's us.

"Tell Mom and Dad I love them and I'm sorry I couldn't face them."

I nod.

"Take care of yourself, little brother." She opens the door with one foot out the door. "Take care of each other." She exits and shuts the door behind her.

I sit in the parking lot, watching her cross the lot and straight into the arms of the guy. He rushes her over to the bench and my heart breaks for my sister, who just couldn't or didn't love her son enough. I know she loves him in her own way, but not enough to put him first.

Backing up, I take one last look at the girl I looked up to most of my life, hoping it's not the last time I'll see her. Then I speed off down the street to pick up what will soon be my son on paper. He's always been my son in my heart.

Toby's quiet at the table, doing his homework. The shop hasn't been extremely busy so far today, so I bring him over another cookie and a juice I had in the back.

"Thanks, Miss Ava." He peeks up at me and I sit down next to him.

"Do you need any help?" I look at the homework wondering when third-grade math included division.

"No." He pencils in the right answer and I keep focused over his shoulder seeing how intelligent he is.

I swear I was learning how to tie my shoe at his age.

"So, Toby, has it always just been you and your dad?"

Stop it, Ava. Don't pry.

"We lived with my grandparents for awhile. Until Dad could build the house." He pushes over his sheet of math toward me. "Can you check it for me?"

"Um, sure."

As I channel my grade school math and look over his sheet, he eats his cookie and drinks his juice.

"When is my dad coming to get me?"

My eyes shift off the sheet to the door. "I'm sure he'll be here soon." I look over his last few answers and slide the sheet back over. "This looks good."

He tucks it into his folder and places it in his backpack.

Our conversation stalls and I resist the urge to pry about his and his dad's backstory. That's for Dane to share with me whenever he wants. Truth is, I'm not supposed to care. Regardless of what Charlie thinks, monogamous friends-with-benefits has been done before. I'm sure it has. Right?

"Want to help me in the back?" I nod to the kitchen.

His eyes light up. "Yeah."

He stands up, pushes in his chair, and follows me into the kitchen.

"I was thinking about doing some cupcakes with different color batter swirled together like a zebra, or rainbow? What colors do you think I should use?"

He peruses the colors as I pull the dyes out of my container. "Could we do my team colors?"

I rack my memory for what colors his uniforms were.

"Black and orange. We're the Giants."

"Like Halloween?" I ask.

He frowns. "Like the Giants."

"Okay, the Giants." My voice raises an octave to show how excited I am. "First we need to make the batter."

"Can I crack the eggs? My dad never really lets me. Says it's messy."

I look over to him from pulling the eggs out of the fridge. "I'm surprised your dad cares about you making a mess."

After being at their house the other night, it took everything in me not to grab Lysol and a sponge.

Toby doesn't respond to my question, and I find it funny he's so shy and quiet right now. In camp, he was the center of attention, telling jokes and he never stopped moving.

"You can do the eggs and all the measurements here." I pat the surface of my work table. "Any mess is easy to clean up on this table."

I take a last look at the spotless stainless-steel table I just cleaned for the night before grabbing Toby. I've realized people in Climax Cove don't leave their houses after six at night and if they do, they're going over to Happy Daze, not to grab a cupcake, so I've been closing the shop earlier these days.

Twenty minutes later, I've fished egg shells out of the batter, cleaned up spilled flour, spilled oil, but regardless, the batter is ready.

"Now comes the fun part," I say, grabbing the plastic gloves before we touch the dye. "Here, put these on."

His small hands swim in the gloves, and he stares at them, bending his fingers and straightening them.

"Take this." I hand him the orange dye. "Squeeze in a few drops."

He squeezes the container so hard, a puddle of orange accumulates on top of the batter. "Too much?" he asks, contorting his lips into an *uh oh* expression.

"It will just make it that much more orange."

He smiles. We do the same with black and I let him judge the amount. This time he drips in much less, grabs the spatula, and stirs until the batter resembles midnight.

"Now. Layers or camouflage?"

"Camouflage." His lips spread into a smile.

"Then you scoop and I scoop. We'll fill up the cake pans and get them in the oven."

We do just that, five minutes go by and the cake pans are in the oven. While I clean up the mess, Toby helps by wiping down the table and handing me the items to wash.

"Miss Ava?" he asks, sitting down on a stool behind me.

I glance over my shoulder to let him know I'm listening.

"Do you not like my dad?"

The dish slips from my fingers and plops down into the sudsy water.

"I like him just fine."

"This summer, you yelled at him."

"Well, I was mad because I thought your dad acted more like your big brother than a parent." I continue scrubbing the dishes, rinsing them and putting them on the dry rack.

"He's more fun than my friend's dads, that's for sure."

Done with the dishes, I dry my hands on a towel and turn to face him, leaning against the counter.

"I'm sure he is."

He smiles that magical little boy one that shows how much he loves the person.

"He builds forts, takes me on hikes, bike rides, we camped out on the beach and had a bonfire. My other friend's dads just sit in front of the television."

Dane really is more of a hands-on dad than I had originally thought. Maybe because I concentrated on his dates and late-night activities, but the truth is, Dane's only fault is wanting to have a personal life while he's raising his son. Is that really all that bad? Don't parents deserve a life of their own, outside of their children as long as there's a balance?

"That all sounds like fun," I say.

"He's just always loved me." Toby looks up from entwined hands, and a light bulb turns on in my head. He's trying to persuade me into thinking his dad isn't a bad guy.

"How could he not?" I sit down next to Toby, really wanting to give him a big hug, but he jumps off the stool instead.

"What do we do now?" he quickly changes the topic and I want to reassure him that he's an amazing boy who deserves to be loved and cared for. He's not mine though and I can't overstep.

"We could get started on the frosting?" I offer and his eyes widen, his head nodding. "Okay then."

A HALF HOUR LATER, THE CAKES ARE COOLING AND THE frosting is ready to cover when the door chime rings.

In walks Dane, his shoulders not nearly as strong looking as they usually are.

He beelines to Toby, wrapping his arms around him.

Toby squirms and gets free of his dad's hold. "What are you doing?" he asks, and Dane grabs him again.

"I just missed you."

"You saw me this morning." He stares blankly at his dad. His gaze shifts to me and then back to his dad. "We're making a cake."

Dane looks at the table. "Giants. Nice!"

"Yeah, and we're waiting for it to cool to frost it."

"Enough time for us to have a chat. Go grab your bag, I need to talk to Miss Ava." He pats him on the back.

"Chat? I swear I didn't do anything today." Toby starts pleading his case and I cover my mouth to keep from laughing.

"Guilty conscience?" Dane asks, eyeing me over his son's head with a smirk.

"What else would we talk about?"

"Just go grab your bag." Dane lightly pushes him to get moving and Toby's head falls forward as he walks by me.

"Can I still frost the cake?" he asks me.

My gaze veers to Dane who nods. "Yep. As soon as you and your dad have a talk."

The corners of his lips turn up, and his steps move a little faster.

Once he's out of the kitchen area, Dane approaches me, caging me against the counter.

"He could come back in," I whisper.

"Stay out there, Toby, I'll be right out."

"Okay, Dad."

"Better?" he whispers back.

My face goes slack. Even if my body is bursting like balloons the night of the county fair, I will not give him the satisfaction of knowing how much my body craves his touch.

"We still have the issue of the other woman who got into your car to discuss." My voice drips with false sweetness.

"I promise, you're going to get your questions answered, but I have to talk to Toby first. We'll be fifteen minutes probably. You'll be here?" He steps closer and my nipples peak to attention at his nearness. They're practically calling out for him to touch them.

"I will and don't make me regret it." I narrow my eyes, shooting him a warning glare.

He chuckles, his lips hovering over mine. "You kind of scare me."

"Good." I attempt to make my voice not sound weak and wanting.

"It makes me hot though. Has me thinking of you punishing me." A smirk crosses his lips as he breaks the small distance to press his lips to mine.

His mouth meets mine, but he uses no tongue, and he's separated from me before I can savor his taste.

"To be continued." The heat from his body leaves and a chill envelopes my body. "We'll be right back."

Then he's gone and I'm watching him place his hand on Toby's shoulder, walking him out of the shop.

Toby's question rings in my head. The hatred I had for him morphed into like at some point and it continues to move further up the scale. I need to figure out how to keep it from rising any further before I regret it.

"Did the principal call?" Toby asks again as I walk us over to the path that runs along the ocean.

"No. Why are you so worried about that?" I look down at him, figuring he's probably hiding something that happened at school today, but I'm not going to harp on it because what we're about to talk about is much more important.

He shrugs. "Because usually you only make us walk this route when you want to lecture me about something that happened at school or when you said we were moving into our own house when grandpa was sick." His head swivels my way, his eyes wide with fear.

"No, buddy, grandpa is fine. If anything, he's a bigger pain in my ass than ever," I mumble.

"Then what's going on?"

I find a more secluded area right before we get into town because if we venture too far in, we'll be bombarded with people stopping to talk to us.

"Here, sit down." We walk out on the plank and our legs dangle over the edge. The quiet inlet of the ocean seems like a good enough place to tell him his mother doesn't want him.

"So, I talked to a lawyer today and I wanted to ask you something."

I've delayed this talk until Sara signed the papers because I didn't want to rehash the fact that I'm not his biological dad unless I knew what I hope will happen was a possibility.

"What?" he looks over at me, his eyes unsure what this could be about.

"I want to adopt you."

"Why?" His little brows draw together.

"Well, I want it legal that you're my son."

He gazes out to the ocean for a while and I let the words absorb. It can't be an easy thing to deal with.

"She doesn't want me, right?" His voice cracks.

"No buddy, if she could take you, she would. I fought for you."

He looks up at me, his eyes almost amazed.

"Why?" he says in such a small voice I swear I hear the shell around my guarded heart fracture.

I wrap my arm around his shoulders, pulling him into my side. "I think we've got a pretty good thing going, don't you?" My voice is lighter now in the hopes that he'll see the good parts about this, not the negative.

He nods. "What changes if you adopt me?"

"Nothing. Not a thing."

"So, I can still call you dad?"

"That's who I am to you."

When Toby was two, I took him to the park and another kid was there with his dad. He's called me Dad ever since that day. Well, other than the month after we explained to him about me being his uncle and my sister, Sara, being his mom after a surprise visit. My parents and I wanted to make sure there were no secrets. He referred to me solely as Uncle for awhile until one night he had a nightmare and I slept in his bed with him. The next morning, I got my reward of being dad again. Best word in the English dictionary.

"Hey, Toby." I grip him firmer to pull him from his haunting thoughts. "You're an amazing boy and I knew it the minute you were born. I mean, your crying at two in the morning was a little nerve-wracking, but I love you. I've always loved you as my own and I want that documented."

"What if she wants me back?"

Out of all the questions, he has to ask the one that's like a knife slicing my heart open. He'll never be number one in her life, but damn if I'm going to tell him that.

"If I adopt you and we go to a judge and have paperwork filed, she can't take you away from me."

"Was I a bad kid?"

"No. The fact you had more energy than that damn rabbit with the batteries was tiring, but you were an awesome kid. Listen." I turn him by his shoulders so he can look in my eyes and see how serious I am. "Your mom not sticking around Climax Cove has nothing to do with you. She's just free spirited, like a bird that's hard to cage. But, she's the one missing out. I get to spend everyday with you, and it's a gift I don't take for granted."

He nods, still quiet.

"Hello? I'm Mr. Irresponsible, but I haven't been able to leave your side for eight years."

A small smile starts at the corner of his lips.

"So, are you going to let me adopt you?"

"Well, how about that Xbox game?" His lips widen and his gapped-tooth smile emerges, causing a warm feeling to bloom in my chest.

"You're going to try and cut a deal with me?" I chuckle and pull him into my chest, pretending to give him a noogie.

He laughs and I hold him tight in my arms. He may no longer smell like watermelon from his toddler shampoo, and he hardly wants to sit in my lap much anymore, but he's mine. Always has been and now always will be.

"Do you think the cake is cooled now?"

He dislodges himself from me and stands up on the plank.

"That's it. Our conversation is over?" I jump to my feet and he's already starting to walk back to the bakery.

"What do you want? Crying and hugs?" He chuckles and runs because he knows I'm about to chase him.

I catch him before he rounds the corner of Marcus' boat restoration shop.

"I love you, Toby."

He nods. "I love you, too, Dad."

And it's over. The conversation I was worried about is all over. I'm not naïve enough to think those are the last of his questions, but he's accepting me, which speaks more than rehashing the fact that he has a mother who doesn't want him and a biological father not even my sister could identify, which speaks to how hard my sister was partying back then. Hell, probably still is.

"You sure are eager to get back to the bakery," I say. He's walking so fast I can barely keep up.

"Miss Ava promised me I could frost the cake."

"I'm sure she's going to wait for you. She frosts enough cakes everyday, she probably welcomes the break." I finally catch up and fall into step with him as we pass the library.

"You like her, don't you?" Toby asks.

"She's okay. A little ornery," I respond, hoping this isn't going to become our topic of conversation.

"If you ever get married some day, what if the girl you're with doesn't want me?"

I stop us and place my hands on both of his shoulders and squeeze. "You're kidding me, right? Me and you are a package deal. If she doesn't want you, then I don't want her."

He nods, turns on his heels and starts up with the fast walking again, saying nothing in response.

"Are you sure you don't want to talk about this more?" I call after him.

He turns his head to look at me behind him. "No, that's it. I'm good, Dad. Promise."

He finally stops outside the doors and I see Ava's closed the shop since we've been gone.

"I'm going to invite Miss Ava over for dinner, and we'll have the cake for dessert." He opens the door and steps in.

"Why don't we just eat at the grill?" I say, following him to the back of the store.

"Because she made a cake. You should make her dinner." He says it matter of factly and keeps walking.

"Don't go playing matchmaker, Toby."

He turns around, a smirk way too similar to the one I've been accused of sporting more than once. I might as well be looking into a mirror.

Like father, like son I suppose. I can't help but grin back.

LATER THAT EVENING, TOBY IS PASSED OUT IN HIS BED AND Ava is grabbing her coat and purse to leave. I walk up behind her, wrapping my arms around her middle.

"Trying to sneak away? Planning to steal my car again?" I chuckle in her ear and she shakes her head.

"You stranded me here."

"Maybe because I wanted to make sure you couldn't sneak off." The scent of her vanilla shampoo puts my body at peace. "I never figured a one-night stand would steal my car."

She giggles and her purse falls back onto the chair it was resting on. "You ready to talk now?" she asks, the playful tone in her voice vanishing.

"Come." I grab our drinks off the table and escort her by her hand outside.

Placing them on the table, I hold out the chair for her and then sit in my own. Her eyes are on the ocean and the light breeze moves strands of her hair around her face.

"The woman," I pause and her chest heaves with a heavy breath, "is my sister."

Her shoulders relax a bit but she continues to stare out to the dark ocean and I can't tell if she's relieved by this news or not.

"I asked her to come back here," I continue because truth is the faster I come out with the fact I'm not the biological father of Toby, the better.

"Where does she live?" I glance through the glass of my patio table to see her purple nail polished toes wiggling along the rails.

"Where ever she lands, usually."

She nods, catching my drift.

"How long is she staying?" she asks, as though I have a normal relationship with my sibling.

"She already left. She did what she came to do and I didn't want Toby seeing her."

She places her beer down on the table and grants me her full attention. "Why?"

"She's Toby's mother." I let the words fall from my lips

and relief washes over me to have this information out there until her eyes widen in what I think is fear.

She slides the chair out and springs up from the seat, ready to bolt. "Oh my God, Toby's a product of incest?" Each word is short and abrupt as it leaves her mouth.

My entire body shakes uncontrollably. "Holy shit. No!" I push away from the table, matching her stance.

"You just said your sister is your son's mother." She shakes her head, looking right and left as though she's being cornered and looking for a way to escape.

"You have it all wrong."

"Dane. This is not funny. Is this some kind of joke?"

She stays in one spot long enough for me to get my arms around her, securing her to my chest.

"No, not a joke. Toby is not biologically mine."

Her eyebrows crinkle and I realize that there's probably a better way to explain all of this.

"I'm so confused." Her rigid body relaxes in my arms.

"I'm his uncle. My sister had a list of about ten guys who could have been the father, not that she could even identify half of them by name."

"Really?" That sparkle in her hazel eyes that I've loved the past few weeks dims. "That's horrible."

I nod and she wiggles out of my hold.

My arms feel empty the moment she's absent in them. She slips off her shoes and steps down onto the wooden plank that leads to the beach, so I follow her lead.

"So, what is she doing back? She here for Toby?" She wraps her arms around herself as the cooler breeze floats off the ocean.

I grab the supplies from the campfire Toby and I had a few nights ago and bring them over to my fire pit. Lighting the match, the paper is quick to catch and since the wood is dry as a bone the fire roars to life.

Ava sits down on the step, closer to the warmth of the flames and I join her once the fire has a life of its own.

"I asked her to sign over her parental rights." I stare out at the ocean. There were many nights after Toby would go to bed and I'd sit out here drinking a beer and wondering what my life would be without him.

"Why?" she asks.

"Am I that much of a dick that you can't guess?"

An embarrassed sigh floats out of her. "Sorry. It's just I'm a little floored right now."

"That I'd take care of a kid who isn't mine biologically? Or the fact that I want to adopt him to make it official?"

She shrugs. "Both I guess. I mean come on. You don't exactly scream man of responsibility."

"There have been times I've struggled giving up my life for him. Not that he doesn't come first, he does, but I haven't forgotten that I'm a man who wants a life too."

"Some would call it selfish." Her tone doesn't suggest she's judging, simply stating a fact.

"I raised my nephew as my own since I was twenty-six. I've housed him, fed him, and clothed him. If I'm selfish for going on a few dates and getting a babysitter or his grand-parents to watch him then I guess I'm selfish." The guilt I bear is revealed in my rambling.

"Hey." She removes her hands from around her middle and raises them up in the air. "I'm not some."

I knock her shoulder with mine. "You were. You said it yourself. I was more a big brother than a dad. To your point I am. I've had to walk that line between fun uncle and authoritative dad figure."

"I'm sorry. If I'd known—"

I shrug. "That's why people don't. I shouldn't be put on some pedestal for taking him. It was never a choice."

"Look who doesn't want to be the center of attention now?" Her teasing tone and body sliding toward me gives me the sign that her anger from earlier at the bakery has faded.

"Can we talk now about the fact that you thought I'd break a pinky promise?" I nudge her down so her back hits the deck and I'm pressed against her.

"Are you really going to make me apologize again?" Her legs widen and I nuzzle into her, grinding the length of my hard-on against her center.

"Would you like to negotiate?" I ask, my lips casting small kisses to the hollow of her neck.

Her hands fall to the back of my head. "What do you have in mind?"

Her hand grazes down my side and I part from her long enough so she can feel me through my pants.

"Mmm...I like the way you think."

"What if Toby wakes up?" she murmurs and my dick deflates slightly.

I pull back to look into her eyes. "I'm in unchartered territory here. I've never had a woman here with him."

"Really?"

I fall off her, laying down next down to her, deflate from her assumptions of me.

"Man, what the hell do you think I am?"

She rolls on top of me, sprinkling me with kisses. "Sorry. So, sorry. Judgment is over. You're nothing like my first impression." Her body slithers down mine until she's on her knees and her fingers are unbuttoning my pants. "Let me make it up to you."

I sit up on my elbows, watching her pull my cock out. "Well, I'm really hurt. It could take awhile."

That sparkle is back in her eyes as she fists me and licks her way up to my tip. She doesn't hold back—the tip of my dick is pushing at the back of her throat in no time.

"Oh, fuck," I say with a groan.

Thank God, the only light out here is from the fire because although Ava's busy polishing my knob, I'm struggling to relax completely with Toby in the house.

Ava works herself into a frenzy and pulls and sucks my cock in the most animalistic way, I'm halfway to come zone, and my sleeping child is the farthest thing from my mind now.

The soft moans falling from her lips as she sucks and rubs me is my undoing—as if she's enjoying this as much as me.

Such a fucking turn-on.

Ladies—a word to the wise. Whether you like giving head or not, if you act like it's your favorite thing in the world to do, you'll have that man more addicted to you than if you were heroin itself. Or Ava's cupcakes.

You can all thank me later.

My head falls back and my arms feel weak from the euphoria running through my veins. I'm trying to count back from one hundred when she cups my balls and gives them a slight squeeze. They tighten, signaling to her she's got me there. And boy does she.

She pops up off my cock with a smirk. "Come for me," she says and squeezes my length in her hand. She throat-dives onto my dick again and a laugh might emerge from my mouth, but cum shoots down her throat at the same time.

She licks me clean, swallowing with a satisfied moan.

"Did you seriously just command me to come?" I ask as she crawls back up to me.

"I did and I'm glad you can listen to instructions." She giggles, her hair falling forward and teasing my face.

"It's time for me to give the orders." My hands grip her hips and I slide up, positioning her on my lap. "Can you be quiet?"

"As a mouse," she whispers.

"You'd better be or I'll have to ball gag you," I joke and pull her up with me when I stand.

"Well then maybe I should scream a little." Her voice is teasing, but I can't deny that I like the way she thinks.

I hang her over my shoulder, grab one of the water bottles and douse the fire, taking my girl into my bedroom caveman style. Just how she likes it.

"F uck," I mumble to myself, staring out my window.

"Bad word." Toby walks into the kitchen dressed and ready for school.

"Looks like I'm riding the bus with you today, buddy."

"Yeah, no." Toby sits down at the table and pours himself a bowl of Frosted Flakes.

"Well, I have no choice unless I want to ask your grandma, and I don't need twenty questions from her." I pour my coffee, looking again at the note Ava left on her empty pillow.

To My Fav Single Dad With The Groin Cleavage,

Didn't want to be here when Toby woke up. I took your car (yes, I'm laughing as I'm writing this). Like the last time I took it, keys are under the mat in front of the bar.

. . .

Yours quietly whimpering,
   Rode Hard & Still Wet

I grin at the way she signed off her letter, but seriously, the girl has a serious problem understanding that you shouldn't take what belongs to others.

I fold the note in my hand, pocket it, then proceed to cut up a banana for Toby. I finish packing his lunch and stuff everything into his backpack.

While he eats, I pull out my phone.

Me: You should be picking me up.
   Ava: Sorry. Big day at the bakery.
   Me: You better be making my cupcake order.
   Ava: Cool your jets. I'm doing muffins this morning. 😊
   Me: Hmm ... I could use some MUFF-ins.
   Ava: Your mind spends a lot of time in the gutter.
   Me: You're opposed to me eating your MUFF-in?

I imagine her cheeks flushing with the slightest shade of pink.

Ava: You better hurry. I've already had a few men in here who seemed to enjoy my MUFF-ins very much.

I laugh and Toby glances over to me, rolls his eyes, and then shovels another heaping spoonful of cereal into his mouth.

. . .

ME: Who isn't the monogamous one now?

Ava: A girl has to make a living.

Me: I'll be there in twenty minutes and I want your extra sweet, extra juicy MUFF-in waiting.

Ava: First come first serve. 😏

I glance at the clock on my phone and stand so fast, the chair slides to the other end of the kitchen. "We gotta go."

Toby takes a few bites of his banana and swings his arms through his backpack.

The bus is coming down our street as we run out of the house, so I quickly lock the door behind me.

Toby runs on the bus, finding a seat in the back with his friends and completely ignoring me.

Luckily, the bus driver is my friend from high school, Cee Cee. She's a mom herself and took the job of driving the bus in order to be home as much as she could.

"I need a ride," I say from the bottom of the steps.

Cee Cee laughs, her hand resting on the handle to close the doors. "You upset some chick and she steal your car?" she asks, laughing more to herself now as I trudge up the steps of the loser cruiser I thought I was done with.

I slide into the front seat because no one ever sits in the front unless you need a place to put your giant ass cello.

"Something like that. You're still routed to go through downtown, right?"

"Yeah. Want me to drop you at the bar?" She eyes me sitting behind her in the extra-wide rearview mirror.

"Perfect." I sit back and drink my coffee like I'm starring in Driving Miss Daisy or something.

"So, I heard a rumor about you." Cee Cee glances at me through the mirror.

I slide up to the edge to hear her better since the kids seem to be competing on who can be the loudest. Toby's obviously the winner since it's his voice I hear plain as day.

"No, I didn't double park outside Steaming Hotties and get towed," I laugh, joking because I already know where she's going with this.

She eyes me again through that big mirror. "Maybe not, but I hear you've been doing a lot of dropping in at the new bakery in town." She smiles a cocky grin as if she knows each and every position Ava and I have tried out. Impossible —there's too many.

"Have you tried their cupcakes? They're addicting." I pat my belly to show how many I've consumed as of late.

I may be trying to get this conversation to make a detour, but Cee Cee seems hell bent on sticking to her route.

"And her cookies, you like them too?" She smirks through the mirror.

She always was a smart ass with a dirty mind. That's probably why we got along in high school. Birds of a feather and all that.

"Actually, I was just talking about eating her muffins this morning."

Her foot slips on the brake, and we all fly forward, my dark coffee spilling out of the lid.

"I swear Dane, you always did love to try and shock me." She's laughing while her eyes inspect the kids as they grumble.

"You brought up her cookies, I thought we were trying to out do one another."

"So, are the rumors true?" She tries a different approach because I'm sure she wants to be the queen bee who holds all the information. If Ava wouldn't have stolen my car this morning, I might actually have been able to fly under the Climax Cove rumor mill radar.

"Rumors?"

We're stopped at a light, so she leans back turning her head to whisper. "That you're screwing the baker."

"Now, Cee Cee. You shouldn't believe everything you hear."

We're one light away from downtown and the corner she'll let me off at.

"I haven't even asked you if what people are saying is true."

"Meaning?" I scrunch my forehead, not sure what she's getting at.

"That the gorgeous baker hypnotized Climax Cove's perpetual manwhore into a doting boyfriend."

I scoff. "Me, a boyfriend? Come on Cee Cee, use that brilliant brain of yours." I lean back, shaking my head.

Her gaze finds me in the mirror, assessing me as I think over what she's saying. I did confess my biggest secret to her, but is it that big of a secret? The whole town knows about Toby's parentage, it's just not something anyone ever discusses. As it should be.

But you've never once talked about it with a woman you're banging before.

Lucky for me the bus stops, and Cee Cee is kind enough to stop right outside the bar. Unfortunately, I have to get out on the bakery side of the street and Ava is bent over wiping down the tables outside.

"See you, Toby!" I wave and he rolls his eyes, sliding down the seat, his hand barely lifting in my direction.

"I don't know, Dane looks like she has nice buns too."

Cee Cee laughs, cranking the door open for me. "What will I tell the gossip mill?" She pats her finger to her lips.

"Cee Cee, she has nice buns, a fantastic muffin, and her oven rack is to die for, but I'm not boyfriend material, we both know that." I wink and jog down the steps.

Ava turns around, her eyes flashing with amusement as I step off the yellow monstrosity.

"One day, Dane. A woman is going to knock you on that fine ass of yours," Cee Cee calls out after me.

I bend over and wiggle said ass in her face.

The doors shut and her laughter eventually fades begins to move away from the curb.

"Hi, Miss Ava," Toby waves ecstatically out the window.

He can't even wave goodbye to me, but he can lean half his body out the window for Ava? Jeez.

"Get back in the window, Toby. See you later," Ava says, waving to him.

He smiles and crawls back into the bus.

"Well, little boy, would you like a cookie?" Ava asks, in a sweet voice like I'm a toddler.

"I'm more interested in your special *muff*in."

I place my hands on her hips and backtrack her into the bakery. Springing the door open, I shut it behind us and flick the lock behind me.

"Get those buns in the storage room." I smack her ass, and she jumps but obeys.

I change her sign to say she'll be back in fifteen minutes. Would I like longer? Of course, but we'll make this short and sweet. There's something satisfying about knowing she'll be wanting me for the rest of the day.

"I have customers," she says and I glance around the empty room.

"Yeah, me and shouldn't you be aiming to please me?" I cross the room, twisting her around and picking her up.

She yelps and her legs wrap around my waist. A perfect fucking fit.

"I think I pleased you just fine last night." Her fingers twirl the small hairs on the back of my head. I could let her do that for hours.

"That you did, but I'm fairly sure I repaid that favor at about two a.m.?" I squint my eye like I can't remember every time we brushed against each other, waking me up, and one touch led to more.

Which reminds me, condoms. I need condoms.

"I don't remember." A playful smile flirts on her lips and I step us into the storage room and slam the door shut, dropping her on a sack of flour.

"We can't do it on the floor?" she says, and I'm happy that she didn't even fight me on closing her store to have a quickie.

"Lay back and relax. You have one job. I'm going to eat your pussy and all you have to do is come all over my face."

Her face blushes and she licks her lips then bites her bottom one.

"You're even dressed for the occasion." I wink and my hands move up her cute summer skirt, hooking my fingers on either side of her underwear.

I drag them down her legs and fall to my knees. They hit the linoleum floor and I pull her to the edge of the flour sacks.

"Mmm...you smell fucking fantastic as usual," I say while inhaling her delicious scent.

With the front of her skirt covering my face, I get down to business.

"Dane," she pleads after a minute of me lapping at her.

But instead of bringing her the relief she's craving, I torture her and blow lightly on her clit.

Her hips wiggle and I dart my tongue to her clit, play with her swollen bud, and retract my tongue to tease her.

"Dane." There's a warning in her tone, as though she has any control over this situation.

I push my flat tongue along her center and her legs fall to the sides while a low moan escapes her mouth.

Hearing her response, I imagine her eyes fluttering back, her hands gripping the sides of the sack of flour and I stop, blowing again. Her body tenses immediately.

"Dane!" she half yells now.

"You are a demanding little thing, aren't you?" I say against her perfect pussy.

"Will you please finish me off? I'm going crazy," she pleads.

I chuckle into her wetness and do as she commands. I lick, I suck, I twirl my tongue, making it my own little plaything. Just when I think she's there, I insert two fingers into her and arch up to hit her G-spot.

I'd like nothing more than to prolong this, make her squirm and beg for mercy, but we both have things to do.

"More," she pleads and I pump my fingers in and out. Damn, she's wet. My cock grows even more rigid in my pants, pushing against my zipper.

She starts grinding against my face while I flick my tongue then suck her clit into my mouth, signaling she's almost there, like a rollercoaster teetering at the top of the hill.

"Oh my God," she moans and her thighs shudder, locking my head between them and then releasing, locking again and then finally falling open once more. She comes all over my tongue and clenches around my fingers. I swear this woman and her pussy are addicting.

I slowly remove my fingers, come up for air from under her skirt, and admire her lying there like the satisfied woman I want her to be.

"So, not fair," she mumbles, raising to sit on the sack of flour.

I bend down, taking her lips with mine. Our tongues glide, our lips moving in a rhythm we seemed to perfect last night. When I break apart the kiss, I love the fact her lips are swollen and red.

"I told you, I wanted my *muff*in." I weave my fingers with hers and pulling her into a standing position.

"Did I object?" She raises on her tiptoes and plants another short kiss on my lips. "You want a real muffin now since you just worked up an appetite?"

She opens the storage room and then shuts it immediately, flicking the lock. She turns around and her eyes are as wide as saucers.

"What?" I slide by her and try to grab the doorknob, but she throws her hand over my mouth.

Backing us up from the door, she pushes me into the corner.

"My dad is outside that door," she whispers.

Well, that got my heart racing like I was the one who just got off.

"I'm sure you don't want to have the whole I'm-screwing-your-daughter-for-fun talk, so, stay here until I can get rid of him."

Then she turns around, opens the door as I hide in a corner of the storage room, praying he didn't hear her moans.

"Hey, sweetheart. Are you alone?" he asks, his voice echoing into the storage room from the kitchen beyond.

I'm starting to regret the fact that I gave my dad a spare key to my shop. "Yep. I was just stocking the room. Checking inventory."

Their voices are close enough that I assume they must be hovering around the door.

"Ava, should you really be closing the store so you can watch porn?"

I choke on my own laugh, covering my lips and clamping my mouth shut so I don't give myself away.

"Dad!" she screeches. "I was not watching porn!"

"Well, I heard voices and if you're alone," his voice echoes in the small room and I'm thinking he's giving the door one more look over, "that's about all it could be."

"Maybe you're hearing things. I was just doing inventory."

The door shuts and I'm thankful not to hear them talking about whether Ava was masturbating to porn in her storage room because that image just makes me want to be the one masturbating in her storage room and if her dad yanked open the door and discovered me, how in the hell would I ever explain *that*?

I sit in the dark room that smells of sweetness from all the baking ingredients waiting until I'm given the all-clear. Ten minutes later, I'm playing some game Toby got me addicted to on my phone when a stream of light from the kitchen breaks through the darkness.

Ava stands in the doorway, the light silhouetting her perfect figure.

"You can come out, my own little porn video."

I emerge from the corner, tucking my phone in my back pocket and laughing.

"Don't laugh. My dad probably thinks I'm a nymph now."

I wrap my arms around her waist, but she slides away from me, moving to the front door.

"You're mad?" I ask.

"I'm not mad, we just can't in front of the customers."

Again, I look around at the empty room and quirk my eyebrow.

"When they come in." Her voice is slightly bitter and I wonder if her dad just gave her bad news or something.

"FYI," I lean closer, "you were the soundtrack of that porno." I kiss her cheek and she pushes me in the chest.

"Go! Don't you have a job to get to?" she asks, but now she has a smile on her lips.

"Call me." I open the door, turning around and running right into Miss Betty, the town librarian. "Sorry."

"Dane Murray!" she scolds and hits me with her newspaper.

I exchange looks with Ava.

Her dad might think she was watching porn and I might get my ass kicked by the librarian, but that was one hell of a way to start the morning and we both know it.

19

AVA

I stand there looking out the window of my bakery, like a stalkerish teenage girl, watching my crush until he disappears out of sight.

My head knocks on the glass, and I close my eyes as a defeated feeling overtakes me.

What am I doing?

The door chimes and I straighten up, plastering a smile on my face that doesn't reach my eyes.

Cat floats in with paint smeared along her arms and her hair strung up into a hastily made ponytail.

"Guess what?" Her expression is excited so I push the situation with Dane to the back of my mind.

"What?" I choke out.

"I got my mojo back and we're having a party." She walks around behind the counter, opens my case, and grabs a carrot raisin muffin.

"Help yourself," I deadpan.

Needing to do something with my hands, I head toward the kitchen.

Cat follows, propping herself up on a stool, chomping on her free muffin. "You'll come, right?"

"If you have your mojo, shouldn't you be locked in that gorgeous hillside studio your boyfriend made for you?"

I pull out the eggs, sugar, and the rest of the ingredients to prepare my cupcakes.

"I have been. You mean you didn't even miss me these past few days?" She pretends to pout and then places a chunk of muffin in her mouth.

"It's been busy."

"You mean, you've been getting busy." She laughs.

I crack an egg and it drops from my hands, landing in the bowl, shell and all.

"Damn it."

"Well?" she asks.

I look up at her once I fish the shell out. "I don't even want to hear it."

She shrugs, her eyes zeroed in on me. "I'm not saying anything."

The door chime rings and I wipe my hands on my apron to head out front.

"What's up girlies?" Charlie screams into the store, walking straight back to the kitchen. "Except for Dane's dick of course."

I blow out a breath and walk back to the table, concentrating on my cupcake batter.

"Oh, that looks good." She points to Cat's muffin and scurries out to the kitchen. I can hear her open the glass case and she returns with a muffin in her hand.

"One day I hope to have paying customers," I mumble to myself.

"Hey, I'm here to put an order in for a cake," Cat whines

as though I shouldn't give her shit for stealing muffins and cookies all the time.

"And I'm like a walking advertisement for you. I was raving about you last night at Happy Daze. Those Sex on the Beach cupcakes are orgasm quality desserts." Charlie gives Cat a look that says you gotta have one.

"I want one," Cat whines again like she's learned from Lily.

"I'm on a rotation of what to make for Happy Daze, but as soon as I make them, I'll let you know so you can go to Happy Daze and buy one." I give her a syrupy sweet smile then turn on my mixer, shuffling to the cabinet to grab more ingredients for the icing.

"Funny, I'll gladly pay my way." She fishes out a twenty from her back pocket and places it on the counter.

"Put your money away, I'm sorry. I'm just in a bad mood." I grab my scoop and the cupcake trays to get the batter in the oven. I'm behind after the impromptu visit from Dane.

"Did Dane do something?" Charlie props herself up on my counter, biting into the top of the muffin.

"What? No. Oh My God, can everyone just stop with the gossip? Not everything is about Dane freaking Murray."

"Technically, it's not gossip if it's true." Cat raises those perfectly arched eyebrows.

I turn on the mixer again, just to drown out their voices.

Which was useless since when I turn it off, they're both exchanging looks. So, I scoop the batter into the cupcake pan, trying to ignore them.

"What kind of cake do you want?" I ask Cat after a minute of silence thinking maybe I can change the subject to something other than Dane.

"Um." She carefully folds the paper liner from the muffin. "I want something fun and colorful to celebrate fall."

"What's this about?" Charlie asks, her jean-clad legs swinging back and forth.

"We're having a party. Marcus and I." She smiles and I can't deny that I've been envious of what Marcus and Cat share since they got together. Although I'm not ready for the time a relationship takes right now, I'm a little lonely when Cat is at Marcus' and Charlie is at work.

Dinner last night with Toby and Dane was nice if I let myself admit it. The fire, talking on the patio after Toby went to bed.

"Hey," I look at the two of them, each granting me their full attention. I stuff the cupcakes in the oven and turn on the timer. "Did you guys know about Toby and Dane?"

Cat glances to Charlie. Charlie nibbles on the inside of her cheek, something I've learned means she's uncomfortable.

"Yeah," Charlie answers first. I'd already figured she knew since she grew up in Climax Cove.

"And you?" I ask Cat.

She nods. "Marcus told me."

"And neither of you thought to tell me?" I sit on the stool, smashing chocolate pieces off the huge chunk of Belgium chocolate in my hand.

"He told you," Charlie says as a statement mixed with a little disbelief. A smile forms on her lips that suggests what everyone in this town wants to believe. That the baker and the bartender are hooking up.

"Only because I saw his sister in town yesterday."

Charlie's eyes widen. "Sara was here? I swear it's been years since she's been back. Is she sticking around"

"Did you know her?" I ask, ignoring her question.

Charlie's already shaking her head. "No. She's older than Dane, so I was too young. But I've heard stories about her. If you think Dane is a wild child, Sara was...well, she was the typical small-town girl who wanted to escape. Looking for guys that would get her out."

Cat stares on, listening intently, clearly hearing about Sara for the first time.

"So, Dane just took Toby for her?" I ask.

Charlie nods. "At first, she'd disappear for weekends, then long weekends, then a week. As the years went by it became months and Dane decided he wanted more for his nephew."

"Do you find it odd that Toby calls Dane dad?" Cat asks, her chin resting on the palm of her hand now, looking like the high of finding her mojo is fading as sleep deprivation creeps in.

"Toby started calling Dane, Dad, one day and except for a brief period when he first found out that Dane was his uncle he's never deviated from that as far as I know."

"Dane told you that?" I ask, my voice shaking that they share such intimate things.

She hops down off the counter. "He did, but only because I pry. I asked him one night when I was working." She approaches me, placing her hand on my upper arm. "I'm his employee, nothing more."

I scoff. "Oh, I don't care. Why would I?" I shake my head. "Please."

Charlie stares at me for an uncomfortable amount of time. "Just thought you should know. Hey, aren't peanut butter and chocolate Dane's favorites?" She glances down to the frosting I'm currently making and the peanut butter jar on the table then turns on her heels. "See you later, I gotta go to work."

"Bye, Charlie!" Cat hollers and the door chime rings a second later.

"You, go home to bed." I point at her with my spatula.

"I thought you said not everything was about Dane Murray?" Cat asks, standing up from the stool and throwing away her muffin wrapper.

"Shut up."

She giggles. "So, you can do whatever you want with the cake. The party is this Saturday, kids are invited. Just a barbecue before the weather turns."

"Got it, I'll bring the cake with me."

"I'm emailing out the invitations tonight." She stops right before she's about to leave the kitchen. "You know, it's okay if you like him, right? I know we all assumed he was this immature single dad who had no business taking care of a kid, but I think we were wrong."

"He might not be who I thought he was, but he's still not boyfriend material. We both know that."

She gives me a tight smile and then turns around toward the door.

"See you later, Cat."

"See you."

Once the door chime rings, my ass falls to the stool, my body completely conflicted with how this friends-with-benefits has morphed into me wanting more.

No, I don't want more. Dane can't offer me more and my mind has to come to grips with that. Maybe we should stop. I know my pussy would not be onboard for that if she had a say. Truthfully, I'm not either. Never have I experienced sex like I have with Dane. Despite knowing how he learned all his moves he always leaves me begging for more. Only now it's more than just his body I'm left wanting.

20

Charlie walks in, a huge smile plastered on her face.

"What's so great this morning?" I ask her, placing the baskets of condiments on each table.

"I just started my morning with a muffin from Ava." She practically bounces to the backroom.

"Funny, I did too," I smile.

"Ew, spare me." She exaggerates an intense full-body shiver.

A couple minutes later she emerges from the backroom wrapping her waist apron around herself.

"Tell me, what is the gossip around town?"

She looks up from behind the bar as she starts taking stock from last night.

"Well, let's see. Miss Betty is on the warpath for a missing book, little Peter Caldwell peed in the fountain so now there's a debate about whether it needs to be drained or not, and," she taps her finger to her lips, "people are saying that Dane, the owner of Happy Daze should pay his best employee, Charlie, double what he pays her now."

"Charlie?" I sit on the stool on the other side of the bar top from her.

"People want to know if someone finally got you to settle down." She leans against the other side of the bar, sipping a cup of coffee I just prepared.

"How do people even know about us? We've been keeping a low profile."

She lets loose a full belly laugh, bent over exaggerating her amusement.

"This is Climax Cove. Sometimes I'm convinced we live in a make-believe town like that Truman movie with Jim Carey. Where they made up his entire life?"

I shake my head. "Stay on course, Charlie."

"You're over there all the time, you've convinced Steaming Hotties to feature her baked goods in a basket on the counter by the till, Double D's is taking her wedding cakes now, and you tell everyone to go there all the time."

"Because she's a great baker. Her goods taste awesome."

"Well, I wouldn't know about her goods, but her cupcakes *are* delicious." That familiar smart-ass smirk is splashed on her face.

"Do you think Vic knows?" I'm a little afraid to ask. I know it's Ava's call whether or not her dad should know about us but I can't help but feel like a douche for keeping it from him. No, we're not besties and I'm not sure you could even call us buddies, but I do see him a couple times a month.

The smirk wipes off her face. I'm not sure how happy he'd be that a fellow Single Dads Club member would be dating his daughter. Fuck, I'm not even dating her, I'm fucking her. Plain and simple.

"Who knows. He doesn't come down to town very often. Plus, he's never been one to be in on the gossip."

I nod because she's right. Vic isn't usually looking to gossip when he's at the Single Dads Club get-togethers.

"But, Dane, you know this isn't going to end well, right?" Charlie leans forward, her steaming mug of coffee cupped between her hands.

"We've agreed to the terms together, and I've been monogamous for the first time in my life."

"That's why I don't understand why the two of you continue to play this game. You might as well just date. The fact she got you to be monogamous says a lot, don't you think?"

"Exactly what does it say?" I notice the SUV parked outside, so I stand from the stool.

"That maybe she's the one for you."

I laugh and shake my head. "Charlie, drink some more coffee. You're not thinking clearly yet."

Walking over to the door, I see the man opening his passenger door, where a woman with dark hair steps out. She's in a pair of shorts and a blouse, and I'd put her around the same age as me.

I step outside onto the sidewalk and approach the vehicle. "Cole Webber?" I ask with my hand extended.

The woman opens the back door and the familiar sound of kids flows out of the high-priced SUV.

"Dane Murray. Pleasure to meet you." He shakes my hand and glances to who I assume is his wife. "Please excuse us, we made it an impromptu family trip."

"Climax Cove is a great place for families," I say.

"Yeah, my wife already has her eye on the bakery over there."

I laugh, watching his wife unbuckle one kid out of the car seat and then the other one jumps out right after.

"The Mad Batter makes some delicious treats."

"Not that these kids need more sugar, but it will keep them busy for awhile while we talk business."

"You said no work," the oldest girl, whines.

Cole ruffles her dark hair. "Relax, pumpkin."

Cole and his wife share a look of complete exhaustion. I've been there plenty.

"Dane, this is my wife, Whitney, and my girls, Veronica and Zoe."

I hold my hand out to his wife. "Nice to meet you."

"You as well. We have friends that come here often. They always speak so highly of the place. Actually, do you know who Marcus Kent is?" she asks.

"What on Earth do you want with Marcus Kent?"

She laughs and the smallest daughter jumps up in front of Cole until he takes her in his arms. Almost immediately she starts playing with the light scruff on his face.

"He's dating my good friend's sister and I kind of want to meet him."

"Whit, we've been over this. I'm sure he's a fine guy. Cat wouldn't be with a douchebag." Cole's gaze veers to me. "He's not a douche, right?"

"I'm bias, he's one of my best friends. We love Cat by the way. The Mad Batter over there is her roommate." I nod across the street to the bakery and Whitney turns her head.

"Perfect, that's all I really need then. But I want to meet him before we leave."

"Well, we're leaving in three days, so you have plenty of time to stalk the poor guy." Cole hands over the little one to his wife. "Just let me get work out of the way first."

She smiles, taking the little girl from him. She settles her on her hip and grabs the older one's hand.

"I'm exploring, call me when you're done. It was great to meet you, Dane, and I can say in all honesty that if you don't take on Rock Hard Whiskey you're a fool of a business man."

"Whit!" Cole says in a way that tells me this isn't the first time she's said something like that.

I chuckle.

"Relax, babe. He seems like a guy who knows a joke when he hears one."

I nod, smiling at their banter. Judging by the older daughter, they've been together for awhile and it's clear they're very happy together.

He wraps his arm around her waist and pulls his wife close, kissing her cheek. "Love you."

Her face blushes and she doesn't push him away nor does she try to escape his hold. She nuzzles closer if anything and the little girl presses her hand to her daddy's cheek.

"Love you." Then her eyes find mine. "Nice to meet you."

A feeling, something like a hollow abyss develops in my chest watching the two together.

"You, too," I say after her.

After Whitney walks her two girls across the street and I'm thankful that Ava will have a new customer today, Cole opens the back of his SUV.

"I swear when I bring them with me, it's a hassle, but it's nice not to sleep without them at night, you know?"

I dodge his question and grab a box of bottles from him. "Need a hand?"

We walk into the bar, sit down at a table, and move on from a topic that I seem to have a harder time brushing off these days.

A<small>N HOUR LATER,</small> I <small>HAVE A NEW WHISKEY DISTRIBUTOR,</small> <small>AND</small> I'm stocking a few bottles with Charlie behind the bar.

"Would you and your family like to have lunch out on the terrace?" I ask Cole, who's busy texting.

He looks up. "Come to think of it, we should probably feed the kids before we bypass their happy hour and all hell breaks loose." His fingers move on the screen again, a smile present the entire time he's texting.

"Yeah, my son has about fifteen minutes past normal feeding times before the crankiness erupts and we're both screaming." I grab a few menus and nod out to the patio that overlooks the marina.

We both head out there, and I lead him to a table that looks out over the water.

"It's beautiful here," Cole says as he takes a seat.

"Yeah and if your wife really does want to hassle Marcus Kent, he's over there." I point to my friend's workshop a little farther down the shoreline where he restores boats.

"Whit's just acting like an overprotective sister. She's been friends with Cat's older sister since they were young, and I think she looks at Cat like she's her own sister in a way." It's funny to me that he's making excuses for his wife. "Add on the fact she's an investigative reporter and you can be rest assured your buddy isn't hiding anything because she would have already found it."

I chuckle for a second thinking of all the grief Whitney's gonna give Marcus. "So, you know Cat's entire family?" I sit down to keep him company until his family arrives.

"Tahlia, Cat's sister and her husband, Lucas we're close with. I don't have a ton of contact with their parents unless there's a party or wedding. But I will say one thing, Marcus held his own when it came to Bill, Cat's dad." He shakes his head. "Hard sell."

We share an understanding nod. Bill Santora was Marcus' client for years and played a huge part in the success of his business. Luckily, when Marcus went down to San Francisco without Cat to talk to him about it, he trusted Marcus enough to let their relationship run its course without interfering.

"He's got balls not many have," I say. "It's probably because he's such a control freak—better to go in prepared than be taken by surprise."

Cole laughs and nods. "Glad to see it worked out for everyone."

I catch sight of Whitney and the two girls being escorted out to the patio by Charlie, so I stand, holding the chair out for the first lady who wants to take the spot.

Charlie positions a highchair next to the table and Whitney places the little one in, then the older girl hops up on the chair I've pulled out.

Noticing a Mad Batter bag in Whitney's hand, I smile. "Did you enjoy what our Mad Batter has to offer?"

I sure as hell have been.

She giggles, as Cole's eyes widen at the size of the bag. "The Alice in Wonderland theme is so cute. We'll have to pop in again so I can show you." She directs her gaze to Cole.

"I'm afraid we'll go bankrupt if I take you in there again," Cole jokes, shaking his head.

"Please." She rolls her eyes. "Ava, the owner, is so sweet. We talked about Cat and what she's been doing here. Then Ava called her so we're going to have dinner with her and Marcus one night before we leave."

Cole's eyes narrow slightly as he studies his wife. "Please tell me you won't be drilling him with questions the entire time?" He shoots his thumb my way. "Dane is Marcus' best friend."

Whitney sits up straighter, her eyes lighting up like she just spotted the Hope Diamond at Tiffany's.

"Really? Tell me everything." She shifts her weight to the edge of her chair.

I place my hands up in the air. "Nope, not getting involved. I'll leave you all to lunch." I hold my hand out to Cole. "It was a pleasure meeting with you."

He accepts my hand and stands. "Thank you and I promise Rock Hard Whiskey will take care of all your needs."

"Well not all of them," Whitney says and Cole shakes his head with a chuckle.

"Love bringing the family with me to business meetings," the sarcasm in his tone isn't missed.

I turn my attention to Whitney who's now shooting her husband a look. "Pleasure meeting you as well. Come down to Climax Cove during Christmas. It's beautiful."

"I'm thinking about planning a friends trip to come up here for the holidays. Seems like a great town," she says.

"I can't say enough good things about it. Lunch is on the house so enjoy yourselves." I nod and wave goodbye before walking back inside where I find Charlie pouring herself a shot of whiskey. "What are you doing?"

"Trying the new stuff." She downs a shot. "Smooth. I like it." Circling the bottle, she inspects the label. "That guy makes this whiskey?" she asks.

I nod. "Yeah, he started about eight or so years ago I guess. It's a pretty well-known brand. I mean, I've heard of it before, but I guess he's kind of selective about where it's served."

"He picked Climax Cove?" She crunches her eyebrows.

My guess is Rock Hard Whiskey is primarily in the urban high-end restaurants.

"I'm not arguing, he's a helluva lot easier to deal with than my last guy. Plus, they kind of know Cat, and it's nice to keep it all friendly."

"Hopefully not as friendly as you are with your dessert supplier." She laughs, already running down the hall to get away from me.

My gaze veers over to the bakery, wondering what she's doing right now.

The three butter pecan cakes are arranged on the counter in the kitchen, looking too good to eat, each placed on pedestals of different heights.

"I cannot wait until they cut that," Charlie says next to me.

She's wearing a cute dress matched with leggings and ankle boots. Fancier than the usual t-shirt and jeans or shorts I see her in at Happy Daze.

"You don't have to work tonight?" I ask.

"Oh, don't worry. Your man will be there, too. He actually trusted Chad to close up tonight." She hip checks me.

"I wasn't asking because of that," I mumble.

She shoots me a look that says, 'we both know you were.'

I stop admiring my cakes so I can spread the hors d'oeuvres Cat and Marcus have out on the table.

"What's the party for again?" Charlie asks me, grabbing a pastry puff.

"Cat's found her mojo." I peruse everything on the table, but for some reason, I haven't been able to eat much of anything today.

"So, every night I double my tips, I should throw a party?" she laughs. "Ow!" she screeches.

I turn to find Cat behind her, pinching her arm. "Don't make fun of me. I was in a slump for weeks."

"I was joking," Charlie huffs out.

All three of us know she wasn't.

"Thanks again, Ava. The cakes look delicious." Cat peers past Charlie to me, and then takes a sip of her wine.

"You're welcome."

"We really want to pay you," Cat says and no sooner does Marcus approach, pulling his wallet out of his back pocket.

"No," I hold my hand up. "Friends don't pay."

"Yes, they do." Dane's voice brings tingles throughout my body.

Had I been waiting for him to show up? Probably.

He situates himself between Marcus and me, his forearm brushing against mine, scorching my skin.

"Is Dane your manager now?" Marcus jokes.

I look up and Dane winks. "I will be if she doesn't start charging people. Babe," he says and I swear every conversation in a two feet perimeter stops. "You have to take money to stay in business."

He doesn't even notice that he referred to me with an endearment in front of everyone.

"I'm with Dane," Marcus grabs sixty dollars and throws it on the counter in front of me.

"It's flour and sugar, Marcus." I push the money back to him.

"And your time." Dane's hand covers mine, stopping me. My stomach roars with a million butterflies escaping their cocoons.

"He's right, Ava, your time has to be factored in," Cat says.

I stare down at the money and I think about rent and utilities. I've wondered lately if I'll still be able to import that chocolate everyone loves if business doesn't pick up.

"How about I give you a discount?" I slide a twenty out, leaving the other forty on the table.

Marcus doesn't go for it and we all stand there for a moment in silence until Dane grabs it and shoves it down my shirt into my bra.

"You did not just do that," I say, my face heating.

Charlie starts laughing next to me, Marcus is shaking his head, and Cat's pressing her lips together trying not to laugh.

"This way you have to keep it." Dane shrugs, taking a puff pastry and popping it into his mouth. "These are so good," he mumbles over his mouthful of food. "Who made them?"

If my body wasn't trying to cool down from the feel of his hand so close to my nipple, I'd grab him by his ear and escort him outside. Lucky for me, it was only the five of us here and since it seems everyone knows that we're screwing each other, it's not as major of a deal that he felt me up in front of them. I can only hope that everyone around us had already lost interest in us and gone back to their own conversations.

"Miss Ava!" Toby screams next to me, his feet sliding to a stop. Lily almost runs into his back.

"Hey, Toby." I squat down, forgetting about Dane and how I need to lecture him about how social etiquette dictates that he doesn't feel me up in front of other people. Especially when we're trying to keep this on the DL.

"We made the championship!" he screams.

I hold my arms out and he comes into them, letting me hug him. "Congratulations! I'm so proud of you."

I catch Dane staring at our exchange.

"Yeah, buddy, way to go," Charlie chimes in, stepping up beside me, ruffling his hair.

When we separate, he looks over to his dad and then back to me. "Will you come to the game?"

"Of course. When is it?" I ask, setting my wine down on the counter.

"It's next Saturday."

I hold my hand up for a high-five. "I'm there."

He smacks it. "Yay!" He runs off screaming with Lily two steps behind.

"That's great, man, you didn't say anything." Marcus' hand cups his friend's shoulder.

Dane shrugs. "We just found out this afternoon. It's fall ball, but this is a great confidence builder for us next spring."

Dane's eyes volley between me and Marcus.

"You should be proud, too, coach." I knock him with my shoulder and his arm swings around, holding me to him as his heated stare makes me melt like ice cream doused in hot fudge.

The doorbell rings and I step back from him. What are we doing showing affection in public?

Marcus disappears only to return a minute later with Garrett and his daughter Sydney right behind him.

"Hey, big daddy." Dane holds out his hand.

Garrett shakes it, his eyes rolling to the back of his head.

"Hey, Sydney." Dane puts his arms around her in a big bear hug, lifting her feet off the ground.

"Hey, Uncle Dane." No emotion in her tone. Nothing that makes her seem excited to be here much less see Dane.

"Don't be a dud, Syd. I get it. You have better things to do than hang around us old people, but cut us some slack, okay?" Dane's overly dramatic with his hands and eye rolls.

"Where's Toby and Lily?" she asks.

"There you go. They could probably use some supervision." Dane pats her on the back.

"I think they're in the basement," Marcus tells her while wrapping his arm around her shoulders. "Thanks for coming."

"Hey, Uncle Marcus," her tone exactly the same as with Dane. "You're welcome."

Her phone is out of her back pocket in her hands as she walks out of the room.

"Old people?" Cat asks and cocks a hip to the side.

"*You* are the old people." I point to the three men. "We're young and vivacious and energetic and—"

"Living in Climax Cove. Population nine hundred and forty-three, six hundred and fifty of those being older than sixty-five," Dane interrupts, hijacking the conversation.

"Then I think I'll take my cupcake business somewhere else." I stare directly at Dane. A threat he'll not like because the man goes crazy for my cupcakes. And I do mean my cupcakes, not my *cupcakes*.

"Let's not get carried away, okay? I get that you're young-*er*. I'm sure Marcus enjoys how limber Cat is."

Marcus hand slaps Dane's chest and he weaves through us to reach Cat's side, promptly putting his arm around her waist and pulling her into him.

"Don't talk about how limber my girlfriend is, dick."

"Definitely crossing the line, man," Garrett mumbles over his carrot stick with dip.

I glance to Charlie who's been quiet ever since Garrett

walked in and I find her face a flushed pink, eyes glued to Garrett.

"Hey," I elbow her in the ribs, which snaps her out of the daze she's in. "Let's go outside for some air."

"Why am I not invited?" Dane whines like a four-year-old. He looks at Garrett. "We're not cool I guess."

Garrett chomps down on another carrot ignoring Dane.

"You're too old for us." I joke and swing my arm through Charlie's, escorting her to the deck.

"What's with all the carrots, man? You half rabbit or something?" I overhear Dane making fun of Garrett as we walk through the patio doors to the deck.

For the first time since Dane entered the room, I feel like I can breathe again.

AN HOUR GOES BY AND DANE HAS BEEN KEEPING HIS DISTANCE. Charlie and I sit next to the fire pit talking with some of the other guests, mostly all town people. Three guys who work for Marcus, and the new barista down at Steaming Hotties. I wish I could say I knew what the conversation was about, but I don't because my eyes are constantly drifting to the windows, searching for Dane.

A newfound worry begins to bloom as I wonder if he's flirting with someone else in the house because why after an hour has he not sought me out?

"I'll be right back." I place my wine glass on the wooden planked table next to Charlie and decide to use the bathroom. At least that's the story I'm telling myself.

I slide through the glass door, dodging some kids that are chasing one another as Marcus yells at them to stop and head downstairs. Toby leads the pack and disappears through a door, which I assume must be the basement.

Marcus shuts the door, smiling at me. "I bet you're longing for the quiet of the bakery right about now." His beer is tucked between two of his fingers in a casual manner that, if he was anyone other than my roommate's boyfriend, I'd find sexy.

No one can deny that Marcus is attractive. Dark wavy hair that has that tousled and just fucked kind of look. He's got a long and lean body and a swimmer or runner's type build.

"The quiet is nice, but a little more noise might make my bottom line better." I laugh and Marcus doesn't.

Instead the corners of his lips turn down slightly. "I was meaning to talk to you about something. Every time I finish a boat, I usually include a gift basket with an assortment of things from Climax Cove. I'd love to include a variety pack of a dozen cupcakes. Is that something I should order ahead of time or can I just drop in?"

"That's very thoughtful of you. You can just drop in. I can either whip something up or we can take from the display case. I don't think you're rolling those boats off on an assembly line."

He chuckles. "Well, no, that's true. I was also thinking... every year I go to a boat conference, and I'd like to hand out cookies with my logo on them. Could we do something like that?"

I pat Marcus' arm and he stares down at it for a moment before meeting my eyes. "Please don't feel like you have to give me business."

"No." His voice raises a few octaves. "That's not why—"

I shake my head. "You're a sweet guy. I see why Cat loves you so much."

"Really, Ava, you'd be helping me out."

I meant what I told him, he's sweet and I have an inkling Dane has put him up to helping me. Either Dane or Cat, but too many townies have approached me lately with business without someone handing them a flint to ignite the idea.

"There you are." Dane walks into the hallway. "People are falling to their knees over your cake. Go sell yourself." He nods in the direction of where the table is setup.

"I'm sure you've probably already done a good of job of it." Marcus' smirk tells me I'm right about my assumptions.

Dane's been the one walking over all town, pushing people to give me business.

"What can I say? I love her cupcakes." He winks and if my stomach wasn't feeling like a firecracker just went off, I'd worry that Marcus saw him. Then again, the man felt me up an hour ago right in front of him.

"That's not all you love," Marcus mumbles. "Gotta go find Cat, see you two later."

Marcus walks down the hallway, swigging his beer. He turns the corner and then Dane's plants his hands on my hips, forcing me to take a few steps backward.

Before I realize what's happened, I'm propped up on a washing machine with Dane's lips attached to mine while he feels around to lock the door behind us.

His hands are fiddling with my dress, my fingers fisted in his hair. God, he always tastes so good. Our tongues glide together only to make us both more ravenous.

"I need you," he murmurs against my lips on the short break we take from mauling one another.

My legs widen and I use one hand and untie my wrap dress so it swings open, revealing my bra and panties for him.

His chest rises and falls as his gaze sweeps over my body, burning my skin with an invisible flame only he can ignite.

While he's busy drooling, my fingers unbutton his jeans. "Tell me you have a condom," I say, my hand palming his dick.

"Never leave home without them." He digs one out of his pocket right before his jeans drop to the laundry room floor. "Boy scout, remember?"

The fact he carries a condom around raises a red flag for me. I hope it's not for anyone other than me.

"Especially when I know you're going to be within an arm's distance." One side of his lips turn up and you'd think he had a magic button to control me the way his one sentence has me grabbing the back of his head and smashing his lips to mine.

Lost in the lust of Dane Murray, our hands grasp, our mouths devour and I barely take a breath before my ass is perched off the washing machine, his fingers are sliding my panties to the side and his dick fills me up. Keeping us connected, he circles us around so I'm on the counter.

A moan escapes me and Dane swallows down my noises with a red-hot kiss, continuing to thrust in and out of me.

In the laundry room of Marcus' house, I lose all control, screwing Dane while people mill around eating my cake and small puff pastry outside the door. I wish I could say I regret it, but I don't until a knock sounds on the door.

22

DANE

I should've waited until I could have her at home because as I button up my jeans and shove the tied condom in my pocket, I watch her cover her skin up with that thin fabric and I'm wishing we had a little longer to go at it again.

Knock, knock.

Ava's panicked eyes reach mine, her fingers tying her dress together and then threading through her long, dark hair.

We both still and stand there in silence as the doorknob jiggles.

We each point at the other one to go out first, but in the end, I figure I have to man up.

Instead of walking to the door, I swing my arm around her waist, pulling her to me. Damn, I love the way she fits just right in my arms.

My lips descend on hers, my tongue seeking hers immediately. She never denies me, and I can't get enough of the fact she seems like she's in a constant state of want for me.

I catch my breath as my mouth parts from hers. Bending

down to her ear, I whisper, "I'll be driving you home tonight."

She shakes her head. "I have my car," she whispers back.

"We'll say it won't start." My lips brush her forehead and I pull away before the person outside gets too antsy.

A small smile covers her mouth and my eyes take their last chance to scan over her body.

"Tonight." I mouth and then unlock the door, and slide out.

"Victor!" I say loud enough for Ava to hear.

"Hey, Dane." He moves to slide by me to walk in the door, so I quickly step in front of him.

"What did you need?" I ask.

He tilts his head skeptically looking at me. "The bathroom."

My heart immediately relaxes. This I can deal with.

"That's the laundry room. The bathroom is down this way." I swing my arm over his shoulders, walking him down the hall.

"Do I need to ask why you were in the laundry room?" Victor jokes, too familiar with my usual antics.

"Just spilled something and was looking for some stain remover." I stop him at the bathroom, thankful it's empty so I can get Ava out of the laundry room while he's doing his business.

"Yeah, yeah. One day you're going to meet a woman who'll knock you on your ass." He laughs while shutting the bathroom door.

I pull out my phone, and text Ava that it's free to leave. She slides out a second later and heads to the kitchen.

Fuck, why do I feel like I've betrayed Victor? Ava's a grown adult and as much as I wish I could stay away, there's no way I can keep my hands off her.

"Dad!" Toby yells and runs up to me. A few other kids circling around.

I beeline away from the bathroom because that just seems creepy if I wait for Vic to get out.

"What's up, buddy?"

"Can I spend the night?" He's bouncing in one spot, obviously excited.

Do we have some telepathic bond or what because in order for me to manipulate Ava every which way tonight, I need Toby somewhere else. Score.

Then the usual guilt seeps in because I wonder if I'm a horrible dad needing some adult time and leaving my kid with someone else?

"If it's okay with Uncle Marcus, but I'm picking you up early and we're going rafting."

He smiles from ear to ear, heading in the direction of Marcus.

"My dad said I can raft category three by myself." He brags to his friends and although I had my reservations about letting him try a harder category, he did excellent last time.

"Really?" The kid next to him sounds shocked.

I enter the kitchen and there stands Ava. Her face flushed and her hair not quite as perfect as it was in the beginning of the night. I'm about to set my course in her direction when Victor comes in through the other opening and greets her.

"I had no idea you were here." He kisses each one of her cheeks.

"Hi, Dad," she says, her eyes finding me over his shoulder.

"Did you make this cake?" he asks, grabbing a pre-cut slice. Ava waits for him to fork off a bite and place it in his mouth. "One of your best," he brags, and her face flushes more.

"You have to say that. You're my dad."

The two continue a conversation about the shop and how business is. I wait a few feet away, pretending like I'm struggling to decide which piece of cake I want to take, eavesdropping on their conversation.

"I thought we could do something tomorrow." Victor leans against the corner and Ava's gaze shoots to mine.

"What did you have in mind?" she asks.

"Dane." Victor spots me and I grab the first piece of cake on the table in front of me, seeing that it's only a sliver of a piece. Who eats a sliver of cake? That'd be like me licking Ava's pussy once. Never going to happen.

"Hello again." I raise the cake plate in the air. "Just grabbing a piece of your daughter's scrumptious cake."

He nods, a tight smile on his lips.

Shit, he must know something.

It's probably because I used the word scrumptious. When the hell have I ever used that word in my life?

"Her skills are impressive." He takes another bite of his and then sets the plate down.

"I can't disagree with you on that one." Ava's face grows even redder though I wouldn't have thought it possible.

Vic turns his attention back to Ava and I figure this is my opportunity to escape.

I back out of the room, tapping my watch behind Vic's back, mouthing to Ava that she has twenty minutes.

Do I feel a little deceitful where Vic is concerned? Absolutely, but it's Ava's father and it should be her decision whether to tell him or not. Besides, that feeling will pass once I have her strapped to my bedpost.

Two hours later, Ava is strapped to my bed.

Not really, but her hands *are* gripping the bars of my headboard, as my mouth teases her sweetness from her body.

"Dane," she pleads.

My tongue plays with her clit as my hand leaves her smooth thigh to get her off exactly how I know she likes it.

I plunge two fingers into her fast and her back arches, her breasts push up and they're so damn mouth-watering I'm about to leave her pussy for them.

I stay on track and arch my fingers to her D-spot—that's right I renamed it after myself since Ava admitted I'm the only one who has ever successfully found it—and suck her clit into my mouth, burying my face in her center.

Her fingers thread through my hair, locking my head to her as she grinds against my face.

"Oh. My. God." I wait for her muscles to tense and then she collapses on the bed, her arms falling to the side.

I slowly remove my fingers and inch up her sweat slicked body.

"You're..." her words trail off and her eyes fall closed for a moment.

I miss the hazel eyes until she pops them open and licks her lips.

Circling my hips, the tip of my dick teases at her opening.

"Ready for number two." I hover over her and her two hands reach behind me, grabbing my ass and I drive into her without thinking.

Her warmth envelopes my dick and it's never felt *this* good before.

Shit. The condom.

I've never been without a condom in my entire life. This is what I've been missing? Hell, I see why they have to preach so much about safe sex. The sensation of her coating me is out of this fucking world.

"Shit, you feel amazing." My body collapses on top of her, my hands reaching up her arms until our fingers entwine and I hold her to the mattress.

"Dane." She sighs and I remove my mouth from her neck to look into her eyes.

No, no, no. Don't lose yourself in her. You need to be the responsible one.

"Condom," I say and move my hips to slide out. I do not need a Toby two point O right now.

Her legs wrap around my waist and she locks me in place. "I'm on the pill, and I'm clean. If you're clean..."

"I'm clean." I quickly reply. "I'm on the testing route and I've never not used a condom, which you're about to figure out if we keep this up because I'm about to come in three seconds."

She grinds her hips and I slow my movements, relishing the slickness of my dick in her soft flesh.

I'd like to say it takes more than that to convince me, but it doesn't.

Leaning up, my hands explore her tits, tweaking and twisting her nipples. Her head falls back, and I circle in and out of her at an excruciatingly slow pace, but this moment is way too awesome to rush.

Her hands run down the length of my chest, her short nails feeling every ridge. Needing to kiss her, I bend over, leading her by the neck up to meet my lips. Our bodies are aligned, and we're slow and gentle.

Never in all my life have I felt like I wanted to freeze time like I do right now.

She clenches around me and I practically lose my load from how intense that feeling is without a barrier.

"Ava." Her name leaves my lips and it's the first time I realize how weak I am for her. Now more than ever.

"More, Dane. I never want this to end," she whispers, closing her eyes as my right hand reaches around and grabs her ass, arching her hips, helping me get as deep as I can get.

"Me either. You're like heaven." I slip in and out of her.

"You too," she says, inching up on her elbows and I grant her wish for a kiss, which leaves us chest to chest, my hand in her hair as my lips cascade over hers until I work my way up her jaw to her earlobe.

No dirty words leave my mouth, no hard and fast movements between us, no nail scratching or ass smacking. Missionary sex turns out to be the best sex of my life so far.

"God, Ava, I'm about to come."

She tightens around me again and I push back the orgasm begging for release.

"Me too," she pants. "Kiss me, Dane. I want to come with you kissing me."

I capture her mouth, our tongues gliding in a slow dance matching the waltz of our two bodies.

The walls of her pussy clamp down on my dick so hard I end up losing my load in her.

Both our tense bodies still until our orgasms fade and then her back hits the mattress, and I stay on top of her, not wanting to leave her body just yet.

I cast kisses to her jaw and neck, and her fingers run down the back of my head.

Once I soften I draw out and head into the bathroom to

grab her a washcloth. When I return, she's still in my bed, her breathing finally slowing.

"Thank you." She holds out her hand, but I wipe her up, trying my best to be gentle in case she's too sensitive.

After we're finished, I hop into bed with her, bringing the sheet up over us.

"Are you tired?" I ask.

She nuzzles into my arms, her head in the crook of my neck and her smooth leg swung over mine. "Not really."

"You want to watch a movie?"

"Sure."

I grab the remote off my side table and kiss the top of her head.

Something feels different. Something feels like we're moving out of the friends-with-benefits zone, but it feels so fucking good, I refuse to think too hard about it right now.

23

AVA

I pry one eye open because of the stream of light peeking through his curtains. My entire body is at peace with where I'm waking up as I inhale the scent of Dane on my pillow.

One side of me knows I'm being stupid—I know exactly where this relationship is going. Right in the dumpster along with my heart because I want more from Dane than these trysts. I'm beginning to form feelings for him. All right, I *have* formed feelings for him. The one thing I swore I wouldn't do.

He's not the man I agreed to have a friends-with-benefits relationship with. That man was egotistical, self-serving, and a grade A asshole who thought with his dick and not his heart.

I yearn for the side of Dane most don't see. The one who wants to adopt his sister's son, who tries to make sure I stay in business, who coaches his son's little league games...the one who made love to me last night.

A deep voice on the other side of the door startles me and I sit up straight in bed. Grabbing his t-shirt strung over the chair in the corner I slip it on and crack the bedroom door open.

"Vic, listen to me," Dane says somewhere down the hall.

My heart hammers in my chest. My dad is here?

"No, Dane. I heard you with that girl in the laundry room at Marcus' last night. Ava's car was sitting outside his house when I left. I was told that she had car trouble and you agreed to take her home. Imagine my surprise when I go to her house this morning to offer a hand and find out she's not there. Please tell me she's not in your bedroom."

"Vic." Dane's stalling.

"I'm about to barge in there if you don't start explaining." The anger is apparent in my dad's voice, and the last thing I want is the temper from his Brazilian side to make an appearance. Afraid he'll make good on his threat, I shut the door quietly, putting on my dress and shoving my bra and underwear in my purse.

"It's not what this looks like."

Can't Dane just lie? Tell him it isn't me in here?

"I think you're fucking around with my daughter. She's not like your other girls."

Dane's quiet for a moment and I strain to listen at the door again.

"I know."

"You know? So, she *is* in that bedroom?"

I glance at the clock. Eight o'clock and my dad's already up and looking for me.

"Listen, I'm not gonna lie to you. I respect you way too much to do that. If I were in your shoes I'd want you to know. Yes, Ava is here."

Damn it.

"Fuck you, Dane." There's that tone I remember from my youth when I'd do something stupid.

"Vic. It's not like that."

"Like what?"

Hope blooms in my chest as I wait to hear Dane's next words.

"We're friends."

Friends. It feels like a knife just gutted me open.

"Friends? You think this makes it better because you like her as a person? My daughter deserves a helluva lot better than some guy who can't keep his dick in his pants. She deserves to be treated with respect, to be worshiped for the amazing young lady she is."

Dane's quiet for another moment. "You're right."

It's quiet for a moment and I can picture my dad running his hands over the top of his white and grey beard, trying to rein in his temper.

"I think you're a good guy, don't get me wrong. You do so much for this town and no one can refute that. But boyfriend material? You've never even had a relationship that I know of. Have you?"

"No." Dane's tone is downright melancholy now.

"I don't want my daughter to be the guinea pig." I hear his footsteps and the front door creak open. "If you don't think you're ready for this then don't fool yourself into thinking because you're friends, no one will get hurt in the end. I'd put money on the fact that the two of you aren't on the same playing field. Eventually, someone will want more, and my money is on my daughter if she's not already there. Don't be selfish, Dane. Man up or get out."

The door shuts, and the ensuing silence weighs heavy on my shoulders.

I give it a few minutes, but since Dane hasn't come into the room, I head down the hallway, finding him on the back deck sitting in a chair with his head in his hands.

I open the sliding glass door, and he bolts up to a standing position.

"Hey," I say.

"Hey." He walks over to me. "You're dressed already. I was thinking I could give you another earth-shattering orgasm before you leave." He smiles but it's weak and doesn't reach his eyes.

Classic Dane trying to defuse the tension with humor.

"Can we sit?" I ask.

He nods, stepping back and I sit down in the chair across from him, hoping for as much distance as possible.

The ocean is beautiful as the sun shines down on it and water lazily laps at the shore.

"Can I get you a coffee?" He moves to stand, but I signal for him to sit back down.

"I heard."

"Your dad can be scary."

I nod. "He can also be right."

His face loses the usual smile he's known for and he stares me directly in the eyes. That's when I know things are about to change between us.

"Ava."

I shake my head, praying the tears keep at bay until I can hightail it out of here.

"You can't commit, can you?"

His gaze focuses on the table and then out at the ocean.

Guess that's my answer.

"I like you, Dane, a lot and I didn't want to feel this way for you. I wanted to enjoy what you had to offer, but...I lost that battle last night."

He draws in a deep breath and shoves his hand through his hair. "Ava, I just can't. I have Toby and the bar. I'm not the type of guy who can settle down. My schedule is crazy, we'd have no nights together. Soon you'd want something more. Something I can't offer you." He sits back in the chair, shoulders slumped.

"You won't offer me. Not can't. There's a difference."

"I wouldn't make a good boyfriend."

"How do you know? You've never been one," I bite out.

He stares at me long and hard. "Are you trying to convince me? Do you think that I'll cave and be like 'oh, you're right, Ava, I can be a boyfriend?' I've been this way my entire adult life. I know what I want."

"And it isn't me." I rise from the chair unable to continue this conversation.

I refuse to grovel for him only to be heartbroken when I'm still not enough.

"You couldn't be further from the truth. I've never wanted anyone like I want you. Just not as something serious. I'm not built for it. I'd disappoint you eventually."

I roll my eyes. "You sound like a jackass. If you only cared about my pussy, you wouldn't be going around town getting every business to buy from me for one reason or another. You wouldn't have made love to me last night and held me in your arms the entire night. Guys who only want friends-with-benefits don't do those things."

"I agree maybe a line blurred last night, but it was one night. Doesn't mean anything."

The contents of my gutted chest spill out down to the ground. At least that's what it feels like.

"Bye, Dane." I march through the back door and straight for the front of the house, making a pit stop for my purse first.

"What are you going to take my car again?" He follows behind me.

"No. I'll call a taxi." I hit the button for Al on my speed dial and give him Dane's address. Luckily, he's not far.

Without a word, I step out the door and slam it behind me, only to hear Dane follow me out.

We stand there in silence for a few minutes, me refusing to speak to the bastard for fear I'll burst out crying and him...well, him doing I don't know what because he's standing behind me.

"Ava, I don't want us to end like this."

"End?" I turn to face him. "According to you, we never even started. Have a nice life, Dane, stay on your side of Main Street from now on."

Like a gift from the heavens, Al pulls up into the driveway at that exact moment. I rush over to the car, hop in, and slam the door shut.

As Al pulls away, I'm not going to lie, I kind of wish for a movie moment. The one where the man chases down the taxi, admits he was wrong and didn't mean anything he said. Then he takes her in his arms and kisses her until applause rings out.

But that didn't happen. Dane never chased after me. In fact, when I look out the window I realized he didn't even bother to stand in the driveway and watch me drive out of his life, confirming I made the right decision.

Why does the right decision have to be so damn hard and hurt so damn much?

M onday's suck.

The shipment of Rock Hard Whiskey must have arrived on Saturday and of course, Chad didn't inventory it yet. Hence the reason I love Charlie so much more than Chad.

I busy myself for the first hour, logging the bottles in and then spend five minutes checking out Mad Batter through the window of the bar.

She's open. Her door is closed, but the fall weather has finally kicked in full force this morning, and she's probably trying to keep her place warm. Not at all is the closed door a metaphor to keep me out.

I wish I believed that even a little.

The bar door opens, and I'm about to announce we're closed when in walks Marcus and Garrett. I already know why they're here and their scowls don't scare me.

"What the hell is wrong with you?" Marcus is the first to talk, sitting down at the bar across from me.

"Party was great, man. Thanks again for the invite," I dodge his question.

"Did you think she'd never want you to be serious?" Garrett finally opens his mouth and I wish he hadn't.

I toss the dishrag on the bar top. "I don't need to be lectured by the two of you." I disappear into the kitchen, prepping the meat for today's special.

When I decided to add on the grill, I did a ton of research on recipes I could make fresh for large groups. Every day there's one special and usually it's a sandwich with a marinated or slow grilled meat.

The two know-it-alls follow behind me.

"I don't even know what you're talking about," I say in an attempt to put them off. One I know is useless but you can't blame a guy for trying.

"Cut the shit. Everyone in this town knows you and Ava have been fucking around. Now everyone knows that you broke her heart." Marcus is the one with all the accusations.

"I didn't break her heart."

"Did you really think the whole monogamous friends-with-benefits was an actual thing?" Marcus asks.

"What?" I flick my gaze to him. "How do you know?"

"Do you live under some rock? Girls talk," Garrett chimes in.

"Cat is my girlfriend and guess what happens when things go south with you and your girl? She talks to my girl who in turn gives me the back turn last night because my friend is a dick." Marcus' tone grows more agitated. Not that I give a shit, he signed up for the problems when he agreed to date Cat.

I never agreed to date anyone.

"Back turn?" I ask.

"Where you're denied sex at bed time." Garrett crosses his arms and I'm beginning to feel as though they're ganging up on me. His beastly frame has him looking more like a bodyguard at a strip club than a supportive buddy.

"I wouldn't know that move because I don't do bed times with my women." I pull on the plastic gloves and grab my spices for the rub.

"One day, Dane, you're going to realize you made a mistake." Marcus shakes his head in that fatherly way he seems to love so much.

"I'm telling the Club," Garrett says, voicing his own disapproval.

"It's not Fight Club, big guy, they aren't going to beat me up in the corner until I agree to date Ava. Let's not forget her dad is a member."

Marcus puts his hands in the air. "I'm out. I can't take this anymore." He's a man of his word as he walks out of the kitchen and I hear the front door open and close.

Garrett however stays. He not only stays, he takes the stool that's in the corner by the point-of-sale machine that the wait staff use.

"What?" I whine feeling like a teenager who was just caught with his pants down on top of his girlfriend and is about to get the sex talk.

"Marcus is right, you'll regret this one day. I know you think a monogamous relationship is worse than a death sentence, but what do you think is so different than what you and Ava have been doing?"

I throw the meat in the smoker and take off my gloves and wash my hands.

"If we were in a relationship, the stakes would be higher. She'd nag. I'd get bored. Eventually I'd disappoint her like I do with everyone. Sounds like I'm really missing out."

"You are my friend. You just haven't realized it yet." He rubs at his beard for a minute before he continues. "You're missing out on all the best stuff." He runs a hand through the long hair on the top of his head with frustration.

"See." I point to him. "That's where you're wrong. I get the sex."

Garrett lets out an exhausted sigh and though I can tell he's trying not to let the undertow of his memories drag him down, it's clear they are.

"It's not the sex. It's the sharing your life with someone. Movies with popcorn and having her snuggled into your side. Watching the sunset on the deck in each other's arms. Seeing her smile when you surprise her with flowers. Having someone in this world who really, truly gets you. Someone you can look at and have a whole conversation with, without saying a word. Someone you know will be there no matter what life throws at you." He swallows and his eyes go distant for a moment. "I miss it every damn day," he whispers.

"I'm sorry."

The mood in the room shifts and with good reason. Garrett was dealt a shit hand when his wife died.

"Don't be sorry. It happened twelve years ago," he pauses and I see him swallow before he continues. "All I'm saying is don't let a little fear ruin what you guys have. I've never seen you as happy as I have since you've been spending time with Ava."

He stands up to leave and I walk over putting my arms around him.

"I'm sorry about Melissa."

"Get off me." He pushes me off him and steps back with a small smile playing on his lips. "Listen, I may have taken days with her for granted, but I know now, no one will ever compare, and that's why I don't date. Once you have the real thing, everything else is second best." He clasps his hand on my shoulder. "Don't let her slip out of your grasp because you're scared."

"I'm not scared."

He quirks an eyebrow. "We both know you are. Just think long and hard about it."

He walks out the door and then steps back for a second.

"Hey, Charlie," he murmurs, putting his head down.

Charlie walks in right after Garrett's departure.

"Good morning," I say, but all she does is give me the finger in the air and walk into the bathroom.

Great, now I have two ornery females pissed at me. Things can only get better from here, right?

25

I drop a tray of burnt cupcakes in the sink and slouch down on my stool. Maybe I made the wrong decision. Maybe I could be with Dane and not want something more.

The door chimes and I stand up.

Stop feeling sorry for yourself.

"Ava?" Cat walks to the back, waving her hand through the smoke. "Is something on fire?" she asks.

"No. Apparently I've lost all baking ability." I pop the burnt cupcakes out of the pan, throwing them in the garbage and then turning on the water to soak the pans.

"I'm yours all day today." She smiles, moving over to grab her apron.

"No, you're not." I point to the door. "You have your mojo back and you need to work on the pieces for that gallery spot next month."

"Nope. You're stuck with me." She leaves the room and I hear her in the display case fiddling with things. "We need some more goodies."

I sit on the stool again, the side of my face laying in the

palm of my hand. "What's the use? I can't sell anything. Dane's probably been bribing people to buy my stuff. Add on the fact that I have to see him every day through the window? It's an impossible feat."

I stand up and look through the cut-out, my gaze focused on his Mustang parked out front of his bar.

"Nonsense. Everyone loves your baking. I hear people rave about it all the time. Why don't you do something different, get your mind off of him." She stares at me through the open cut-out between the kitchen and the front of the store. "Make a wedding cake."

"Yeah, that's what I want to do, Cat. Make a wedding cake when I'm miserable over a man."

She's in the kitchen, at my side a second later.

"It's his loss." She wraps me in a warm hug and the prickling of tears stings the corner of my eyes, and I try to push it back.

"I'm stupid. I mean did I honestly think that the playboy of Climax Cove would ever settle down?"

"You're not stupid. You didn't mean to fall for him. You were having fun, but you're just not that type of girl. Hell, I don't think there's a girl out there who can't not develop feelings for a guy she's sleeping with on the regular. Women are built differently than men and there's nothing wrong with that."

Cat, forever the optimistic one.

"I just want to smash something," I say, clenching my fists at my side.

I glance down at the heart cookie I was making for sweetest day this weekend and before I realize what I'm doing, it's crumbling in my hands.

"Okay, Ava." Cat pries my hands open and the crumbs fall to the counter. "Let's channel this anger into something productive. Why don't we bake? You always seem calm when you bake."

I glance to the sink with the burnt cupcake pans. Her gaze follows mine.

"Let's not do cupcakes. Let's dip things in chocolate or something."

"I'm a baker, not a chocolatier," I remark and she huffs, clearly annoyed with my woe is me attitude.

"Then let's bake things and smash them."

Her sentence gives me an idea and I could kiss her. I run to the backroom, finding all the supplies and piling bags of sugar candy and pounds of chocolate on the table.

"I'm loving this inspired look you have going on right now." Cat's finger circles around my face. "What are we making?"

"I'm making piñata cakes. Could you do me a favor and run down to Nail Me Hardware and get some small wooden hammers? If they don't have wood, get the smallest ones and pretty duct tape."

She looks at me like I'm literally growing a third head.

"Please, Cat. You'll understand once I'm done."

For the first time in twenty-four hours, Dane isn't on my mind.

Progress. At last.

News got out quickly after the first mother and daughter duo stopped by after school and saw the small piñata cakes. A layer of chocolate or vanilla cake, domed in chocolate with sugary treats relieved once you break open the chocolate.

A line is beginning to form for the first time outside the bakery. Kids and adults wanting to get my latest creation.

"I need more." Cat's eyes bug out of her head, and Lily sneaks in taking a handful of hammers.

"Thanks for helping, Lily. I put a special one aside for you." I eye the rainbow candy dome in the corner. She smiles and I'm sure it takes everything in her not to break it open.

"Thanks, Miss Ava."

She disappears into the front of the store and I carefully place Skittles and chocolate gold coins on top of the cake, positioning the chocolate dome over the top of it.

In the corner of my vision, a head pops around the corner with a mop of messy hair and warm caramel eyes as warm and inviting as his dad's green ones.

"Miss Ava?"

"Come on in, Toby." I wave him over, stepping away to wash my hands.

"These cakes look awesome." He eyes the trays lined with piñata cakes. The only baked good I've managed to make today.

"Thank you. Would you like one?" I ask, grabbing one from the tray and placing it on a plate.

"Ya, thanks." His backpack is still swung over his shoulder.

"Did you just get back from school?" I hand him the small hammer.

"Yeah."

"You can take the cake over to your dad's work if you'd like."

He shakes his head. "Are you coming to my game this weekend?"

My shoulders sag. I forgot about his championship game

I said I'd go to. The thought of sitting on bleachers with Dane only a few feet away weighs in my stomach like an anchor.

"Of course. What time is it?" I plaster a fake smile on my face.

"It's at noon."

"Okay, I'll be there."

His smile only grows and I can suck it up with Dane for one afternoon for Toby's sake.

"Now, smash that cake," I say.

He grabs the hammer and his teeth bite down on his bottom lip. The first time he doesn't crack the chocolate so he goes at it a little harder the second time and it cracks open with small baseball bubble gum spread out over top of the cake.

"Whoa!" he picks one up and pops it in his mouth. "Thanks, Miss Ava." He climbs down from the stool, rushes over and hugs me.

My hand lands on his back. Toby doesn't show me a ton of attention, but this hug feels so good, I'm not ready to let him go yet.

"Anytime. Maybe we can make one together some time."

He steps back, his eyes wide. "Really? Even with my dad being a jackass?"

"Toby," I sigh, crouching down to get eye level with him. "Where did you hear that?"

"My grandpa. He said my dad's being a jackass because he let you go."

I do my damndest to suppress the smile trying to curve my lips.

"Well, sometimes people just don't work out. It's not your dad's fault and it's not mine. We just aren't a good fit."

"But you'll let me bake with you still?" His eyes hold so much hope that even if I didn't intend to, I'd say yes anyway.

"You are welcome here anytime you want." This time I initiate the hug and it might be my imagination but his arms are a little tighter around me.

It's right now that I realize, I didn't just fall for Dane, I fell for Toby, too, and what was left of my diseased heart shrivels up and dies.

"Miss Ava is here!" Toby runs out of the dugout, right into her arms.

Since when did those two get that close?

The clipboard is limp in my hands as she hugs him tight and then she kisses the top of his head. Toby smiles and runs back in the dug out while Ava takes a seat on the bleachers with a pink box in her hands, not even sparing me a glance.

"Dad, did you say hi to Miss Ava?" Toby says, grabbing my hand, beginning to pull me out of the dugout.

"Toby, I have to get the team ready."

"Come on Dad, she made us something. I saw the pink box."

Before I know it, I'm standing in front of her. The girl I've fallen asleep dreaming about and woken up with a hard-on for since the last time I saw her.

"Oh, hey Dane." She sounds surprised and not at all affected as I am by being this near to her.

"Hey, thanks for coming." I roll back on my heels. Toby's

head looking from her to me and back to her like he's expecting something.

"What's in the box?" Toby breaks the uncomfortable silence.

"Cookies. Baseball ones." She opens the box, granting him a smile that used to make my chest feel light when she gave it to me.

Inside the box are baseball cookies for each boy with his name and number.

"Oh, awesome!" Toby reaches in, but Ava closes the lid before he can grab his.

"For after. A congratulations on the win." She winks at him.

"We haven't won. The Cardinals are a tough team. They have the home run hitter."

"Oh, I don't believe they're better than you and the Giants."

She crosses her legs and I notice her outfit for the first time. She's in jeans and a hoodie and somehow looks as good as when she'd strut around in her bra and underwear in front of me.

"Well, we better get to warming up." I place my hand on Toby's shoulder, pulling him to my side. "Thanks for coming."

Just when I'm about to walk away, Charlie climbs the bleachers and takes a seat next to Ava.

"Hey, Toby, you're gonna to rock this game. Point to the fence before you bat." She laughs and I shake my head.

"Way to make him look cocky and arrogant," I remark.

She lifts the box. "Like father like son, right? Maybe he'll die alone like his father will, too."

Fucking A. Seriously, she's going to hammer this shit she's been spouting all week in front of Ava now?

Charlie leans over and looks in the box. "Baseball cookies. Does this mean we can go back to the Eat Me cookies instead of the broken heart ones?"

Ava scoffs. "Charlie." She glances at me and her face flushes that beautiful pink color it would when I'd kiss her sometimes.

Charlie looks up to me. "Oh, sorry." Although her apology sounds genuine, I can tell Ava is mortified.

Not sure why? This is Climax Cove and things get around this town. I've known about her piñata smash cakes, two halves of a heart cookies, and how she's purposely declared the week, red free, using black icing instead.

I get it, I hurt her but I wouldn't change what happened between us. One thing Garrett got right is that I enjoyed my time with her more than any other girl. I regret the hurt she's going through now, but it's just better this way. Eventually, things won't be so awkward.

"Well, we better get going." I place my hand on top of Toby's hat and he runs off into the dugout.

"Go, Giants!" Charlie pumps her fist in the air. "FYI, I'm only cheering on Toby and his teammates. Not you."

I can't believe I take this much shit from my employee. If her brother and I weren't friends I might actually be able to fire her.

Ava pulls out her phone, burying her head in it.

"Good to know. Obviously, you're forgetting who signs your paychecks." I hide in the dugout, watching the rest of my friends sit down on the bleachers next to Ava.

The umpire calls me out to home plate, I shake hands with the Cardinals coach and when I walk back to the dugout, I can't help but let my gaze wander over in the direction of Ava. It's all I can do to keep walking forward because there she sits with my mom right next to her.

THE GAME IS OVER TWO HOURS LATER WITH A WIN FOR US, thanks to Toby's catch at shortstop and getting our third out in the game.

All the players gather their things and grab a cookie from Ava who is handing them out before they scurry off to their moms and dads.

"Thanks again for the cookies," I say to Ava.

"Here." She hands me a cookie with Coach on it.

"Thank you." My eyes instinctively close when I take the first bite. The woman has talents that extend far outside the bedroom.

"You're welcome. Congratulations." She smashes the box and then disposes of it in the recycling bin, and grabs her purse from the bleachers where all of what I guess are now *our* friends sit.

I never realized how interconnected our lives are until I see Cat swinging Lily around in circles, Charlie talking to Sydney and Marcus and Garrett shooting the shit. My parents stand, my dad talking to a couple of the other grandparents at the game.

"Dane," my mom approaches, swinging her arm through mine. "How come I never met Ava? She's wonderful." She thinks she's whispering, but based on the fact that Ava's turned around and that pink flush to the apple of her cheeks, she heard.

"She is," I agree, watching the pink turn full out red.

"Then how come you've never said anything?"

Are my mom and I close? Yeah. But she knows nothing about my female companionship and I think I'll keep it that way.

"Celebration at the bar!" my dad yells and the kids go crazy.

"Dad?"

I have nothing set up for a group this big.

"This is what's great about owning your own place." He clasps me on the shoulder. "Why did you put that arcade in for anyway?"

He walks past me to his car. My mom gives my forearm a tight squeeze and knowing eye and then follows my dad.

"I'm going with grandma," Toby screams and runs after my mom. I wait by my car to see her wrap her arm around his shoulders, leading him to the car.

My eyes search the parking lot, and all that's left of Ava are her taillights driving away.

Suddenly, alone doesn't feel as good as I thought.

LATER THAT NIGHT, I'M IN THE OFFICE GOING OVER ORDERS and shipments when a knock sounds on my door.

"Come in."

My dad steps in and the hope that had my heart beating extra fast falters seeing that it's not her.

I'm surprised he knocked. Usually he barges in with a comment about how it was his office first.

"Mind if we talk?"

"Are you asking me permission?"

"Cut the bullshit." He closes the door and sits down across from me.

"I thought you and mom left."

"Your mom and Toby are watching some Galaxy movie, so I came back when I saw you weren't home yet." He leans back in his chair, his ankle resting comfortably on his knee.

Some say I'm the younger version of my dad. He's tall and although his daily workouts have been exchanged with scenic walks, he's fit and I wouldn't want to run into him in a dark alley.

I remain silent because I'm still baffled by him initiating conversation and the fact that he didn't start it by questioning a decision I've made with the bar.

"I've been hard on you," he pauses for a second, seeming to collect his thoughts before he continues. "Your mom knocked me on the forehead today and I realized that maybe I've failed you in a way."

"Failed?" I ask, a little stunned to hear these words coming from my dad's mouth.

"Made you question yourself and what you can handle." He diverts his gaze from mine.

"I don't think I lack in self-confidence," I say in the cocky way I'm accustomed to.

He chuckles. "Not to others, no. But I think maybe when you're alone you do."

I say nothing. Mother's intuition is never wrong.

"Listen. I'm not into this heart to heart, psychoanalyze every little thing bullshit. I just want you to know, I appreciate you taking over the bar, keeping it in the family. And though you've made some questionable decisions—"

"Gee, thanks, Dad."

His gaze meets mine. "You've made good ones too. Not only with the bar, but with Toby. You could have run off like Sara."

"You know I love Climax Cove."

He nods. "I saw Sara in town. Did she not want to see us?" There's a sadness to his voice I haven't heard in years. In general, we don't talk about my AWOL sister, ever.

My chest tightens. I had wanted her in and out as fast as possible.

"We were just taking care of some business."

"The adoption? She signed the papers?" I can see the agony my sister's choice of lifestyle has had on my father. It's probably given him the majority of his gray hair.

"She did."

He nods his head a few times slowly, his eyes on the floor and his mind far, far away.

"Well, that's done then."

My dad's never been one to talk about his feelings.

"Last thing. You're a good man, Dane, and I'm proud to be your father. I'm not sure why you can't find a woman to settle down with. Why you insist on not giving Toby a mother figure in his life, but your mom says you think you're not good enough. So, I came here to tell you, that you are. Good enough."

"Thanks, Dad." It's strange. I've longed to hear my dad say something along these lines most of my adult life, but now that he is I find I have a hard time accepting it.

"Well, your mom likes the cupcake girl. She thinks she's the one."

"She had one conversation with her," I deadpan.

My dad chuckles again. "Son, you of all people know your mother. She's been seeing you and her a lot more than you think."

God, my parents' house is pretty close to mine, I can only hope to hell my mom didn't see Ava between my legs on the deck.

He knocks on my desk. "I'll try to be more encouraging with what you've done here. It's hard to see everything you built change with the times. Reminds you you're getting old. Because whether you like it or not, Dane, time doesn't slow down. Life will just pass you by if you let it." He smiles and then he's out the door before I can even respond.

My dad leaves the door open on his way out.

"Good night, Mr. Murray," Charlie says as she passes by my office and flips me the bird. "Good night, jackass. Front end is closed."

My mind is swirling with everything I said to Ava, everything she said to me, and everything everyone else has been saying since we split.

The spreadsheets are a blur for the next fifteen minutes while I try to process it all, but the roar of a fire truck breaks through the silence, sounding so near it has me sliding my chair out to inspect on what's going on.

I figure it has to be some drill the fire department was conducting, or maybe some false alarm, but when I get out to the bar area and look out my front window, the one truck Climax Cove owns is parked outside my place, and firefighters are busting down the door of the Mad Batter.

My heart's never felt squeezed so tight. I'm surprised it didn't pop out of my chest.

I was happily enjoying my sulk fest in my bed with a bag of potato chips when I heard the sirens. In the months I've lived here full-time, I'm not sure I've ever heard them before.

My phone vibrates a second later and I glance over to see my dad's name on the screen. Again. Figuring I can't continue to avoid him any longer I slide my thumb over the screen, propping the phone in the crook of my neck continuing to move my hand from the bag of chips to my mouth.

"Where are you?" His voice is panicked.

"In bed."

"Thank goodness. Ava, I need you to come down to the bakery."

I sit up. "Why?"

Rubbing the remnants of salt and vinegar on my yoga pants, I stand up to look out the window to see if I can see anything in the downtown area, but except for the red lights in the dark night sky, nothing.

"Just please. I'll meet you there."

"Dad, is this because of the sirens?"

A long stream of breath is the only thing I hear through the line. "All I know is Hank from Nail Me called and said he saw smoke coming out of the building, but no flames."

"What? I gotta go."

"Av—"

I click my phone off, and I'm running down the stairs when Charlie walks through the front door.

"Where are you going?" she asks.

I whiz by her right out the front door, stopping briefly to throw on my chucks.

By the time I reach downtown the entire street is filled with people, the windows and door of my bakery shattered. My footsteps slow outside the circle of people, gawking like the rest of them at the scene in front of me.

A warm arm wraps around me and my head falls to their shoulder for the comfort.

"Oh, Ava." Charlie's hand rubs up and down my arms. "We'll fix it."

I hadn't even realized she'd followed me in my panic to get here.

Unable to watch my dreams go up in flames in front of my eyes, I bury my head into the crook of her neck. She soothes my cries, but a few minutes go by and her body tenses, all movement stopping.

"What is he doing?" she murmurs.

"Did you find her?" Dane's voice rings through the noise of the spectators and my head lifts to find him covered in soot panic over every one of his features as he yells in a fire-fighter's face.

"No. I don't think she's in there."

"Did you check the storage room? She's here night and day." He moves to run back into the building.

"Dane!" Charlie screams and Dane looks over, relief immediately washing over his face.

He runs over, causing everyone's eyes to follow his movements.

"Thank God." He pulls me into his chest, his hand weaved in the strands of my hair pressing me to him. "I thought you were in there."

I shake my head the little bit I can.

"Dane?" Charlie asks and neither one of them say anything, but I feel the shake of his head. "Did you go in?"

"I went in to find her." He steps back, his two hands wrapping around my upper arms, inspecting me as though he just saved me from the building. "You okay?"

I step back, his hands falling off me. "I'm fine." Walking by him, I weave through the crowd of people to the fire truck, but I'm stopped at the yellow caution tape. I dip under and try to put the fact that all the teacups and pots are now black, out of my mind.

"Excuse me," I ask the man directing the other firefighters.

He stares down at me. "You shouldn't be here. It's dangerous."

"That's my shop."

"I know." His gray beard says he probably knows everyone and everything that happens in this town. "I'm glad to see you weren't in there."

"What's the cause of the fire?" I turn to see Dane right behind me.

"Dane. I already told you to get out of here," the firefighter snaps.

"Jim, you know I'm not going anywhere."

Jim exhales a long and annoyed breath, his eyes never leaving Dane's until they slowly turn toward me.

"We'll have a full report in the morning. From the amount of smoke, you need to wait until the morning to go in. We'll board up the windows for you, and lock it up once we make sure it's out."

"Jim?"

Dane's hands land on my shoulders, squeezing them, standing so close his strong chest is supporting me.

Jim rolls his eyes. "If I had to guess I'd say it's electrical."

Dane's hands leave my shoulders and I hear his groan. "Did you not call an electrician?" he asks me.

"Can I give you my phone number?" I ask Jim, purposely ignoring Dane. I'm not even sure why he's here. He made himself pretty clear, and the way he's acting right now screams boyfriend.

"That would be helpful." He takes out his clipboard and clicks his pen. "Go ahead."

I ramble off my phone number and then take a look at the store, not ready to leave.

"Come into the bar," Dane urges, his arm wrapping around my shoulders again.

"No thank you," I mumble, making my way to Charlie who's sitting on the curb outside the bar.

She stands when I approach, her gaze moving between me and Dane.

I sit down next to her and watch the firemen go in and out of the bakery. The crowd slowly departs, all the local town folks stopping by our threesome to convey their sorrow for my situation.

"Ava," my dad says, crouching down in front of me. "You're okay."

I nod, my eyes unwilling to leave the scene in front of me.

"They think it was electrical," Dane adds in his two cents from next to me.

"I knew we should have gotten that building better inspected." He turns around to watch the firefighters like the rest of us.

"Come in and I'll make you a drink," Dane says next to me, his hand landing on my knee.

I slide my leg over to shake it off.

"I need to talk to you," he murmurs in my ear.

I shake my head.

"I'm going to talk to Jim and see what else I can find out," my dad says to no one in particular and heads in the direction of the fire truck.

"I thought I lost you," Dane whispers, or at least must think he whispered, but Charlie takes her cue and stands up, brushing her ass off.

"I'm going to join your dad."

Charlie walks away, and Dane takes me by my shoulders forcing me to look at him.

"I'm sorry, Ava."

"Thanks. Like everything else in my life, nothing goes as planned, but I'll get through this. Just might take awhile..." Another loud bang inside has me turning my head.

Dane's hand cups my cheek and he directs my head back in his direction.

"No, Ava, I'm sorry for being a jackass." His eyes are tender and overflowing with sorrow. But I'd have the same reaction if his bar were currently burning to the ground.

"Okay." I begin to rotate my neck back around to face the building, but his hand pressures my head to stay in place.

"I want another chance. When I thought you were in there...I couldn't breathe. I ran in before the firefighters, searching every space for you. When I didn't find you, I panicked. My heart sank to the pit of my stomach, and I swore to myself if I found you, I'd never let you go." He grabs me and pulls my limp body into his.

I don't reciprocate the hug. Instead, I lay unmoving in his arms, trying to process why he feels as though now is the time to tell me this.

I'm shoved back upright and he's looking at me like he's expecting an answer to his declaration.

"What do you want me to say?"

"I don't know. Accept my apology."

A laugh escapes before I can quiet myself. "Oh, you're serious." I stand up, brushing the dirt off my ass. "Always so selfish, Dane. You thought I was dead so now you want me?" I stare down at him. "I'm not a shelter dog, Dane, I'm not going to wag my tail and jump in your lap because you rubbed my belly a couple of times."

I walk toward my dad and the fire chief. Charlie glances between me and the curb where I can only hope Dane has disappeared from.

"Ava!" His deep voice rings in the night air, but I keep walking. "Mad Batter!" he yells again and this time Jim, my dad, Charlie, along with all the Climax Cove volunteer firemen are staring in his direction. I turn on my heels, ready to give him the evil eye with the hopes he disappears. "I *will* convince you that you're meant to be with me."

I roll my eyes turning around.

"Seven days from now you'll be in my arms."

"Dane." Charlie's tone is one of warning. "Now isn't the time."

"Even so, it's a promise I intend to keep." His voice seems to get louder as he continues, so I put my hand up in the air, giving him a wave to say *whatever, just go away*.

My dad's ears perk up like a Doberman and he sets his

sights on Dane. "He hurt you?" he asks me, bringing his gaze back around to me.

"No."

With the smoke dying down, most spectators have left, leaving the four of us the only people other than the fire department.

"He did." He steps off the curb to the street, headed toward Dane.

"Whoa, Vic, settle down," Dane says.

Following my dad's path, Dane holds up his arms in the air and the fear in his eyes would normally make me laugh, and a small part of me is saying 'go daddy, kick his ass.'

"I told you someone was going to get hurt and it was my little girl." My dad's finger is already pointed and ready to poke Dane's chest.

Now, Dane is still taller and overall bigger than my dad, but that Brazilian side of his temper is no joke.

"I just confessed to her how much I need her."

"Ohhhhh," Charlie coos next to me. She might as well wear a Team Dane pin on her shirt.

My dad's footsteps stop and he turns to me, looking to me to see if this statement is true.

"I guess once he thinks I'm dead, it makes him realize what he passed on." I cross my arms over my chest.

Dane ignores my dad and steps down off the curb on his side, his gaze locking with mine.

"I love you, Ava Pearson. Yes, it took me until that fire to realize how stupid I was, but I know now. I always was a slow learner."

His footsteps are closing the distance between us and my heart is cracking open, begging me to let him nestle into that empty spot designated for him. Then the devil lands on my right shoulder and I'm reminded of the heartache he's put me through. The fact that he didn't care about us until he thought he could never have us again.

"Fear is ruling your emotions right now, Dane. Tomorrow when you wake up and realize, I'm here and I'm fine, you'll go back to only needing one thing from me and that one thing is just a tiny piece of what I have to offer the man in my life."

"You're wrong."

He steps up, and we're practically chest-to-chest.

"Then you'll have to prove it to me." I grab his wrist and turn his watch to both of us. "Only time will tell."

I walk over to Charlie who wraps her arm around my shoulders, sheltering me from him. He's finally said the words I've longed to hear from him, but with everything going on I can't even deal with it right now.

Either that, or it's too little, too late.

28

AVA

Day One

I stayed until two in the morning. Jim allowed me to walk through quickly after he'd done his investigation with him at my side and a helmet on my head. The damage isn't extensive, mostly just smoke damage, but enough that I'll be closed for awhile.

With a cup of coffee from Steaming Hotties and a baseball cap on my head, I head to the bakery to meet the insurance guy before lunch. I had to call Norma, the building owner last night. She was none too pleased to hear about the fire. Somehow, I managed not to point fingers that maybe she should have looked into the electrical panel I was asking about last month.

Marcus' truck, Garrett's truck, and Dane's Mustang are all parked outside the bakery, the three of them not in sight. I glance over to Happy Daze, seeing it dark and locked up still.

My foot leaves the curb to cross the street and echoes of hammering and sawing ring in the early morning street.

Hank from Nail Me is walking down the street with a flatbed of lumber and drywall.

No. No. No.

By the time I reach the door, I find a crew of six people inside, three of whom are the men who own the vehicles parked out front, all hard at work inside.

"Dane!" I yell.

He walks out from the storage room area, his white shirt sticking to his skin and his pants swung low with his tool belt hanging off his hips.

I hate to admit it but that look really works for him.

"Good morning. I had made you some coffee, but better bet on Steaming Hotties." He winks and leans back on the counter that's still intact.

"What are you doing? The insurance guy is on his way."

"Tom was already here. Took care of that and he gave me the okay to get working. Time is money and we need to get you reopened."

I step closer. "I needed to get estimates and find out who I can afford."

"Tom said he'll be by later with a check. And we're free of charge, so I'm pretty confident that we would've won the bid." He winks and those moss-colored eyes draw me in.

"You aren't doing this for free."

He crosses his arms, his biceps bulging as the sleeves of his t-shirt rise, a classic you can't stop me smirk on his lips. "Just go have some coffee and write down the color of paint you used." He nods over to the prep table in the kitchen, set up with a cup of coffee, a muffin, and a paint wheel.

"You think this is going to win me over somehow?" I cross my own arms and jut out my hip.

He steps closer, his voice lowering into that deep timber

that sends shivers up my spine. "It's only day one. I still have six more, remember?"

Without another word, he turns on his heels and heads back to work.

Day Two

THE USUAL CREW IS AT THE SHOP. MARCUS, GARRETT, SOME guys from Garrett's crew, but today Dane's Mustang is missing. As much as I want to be unaffected by the man and anything he does, it hitches when I notice that he's not here today.

With the front windows on order, they're concentrating most of their efforts in the storage room where all my supplies and ingredients were destroyed.

I sit at the prep table, looking over my list of everything I need to do in order to get the store up and running again when Dane walks in from the back room.

"Good morning. I didn't hear you." He sits on the stool across from me.

Again, with the sweat soaked shirt. Add on the backward baseball hat and I'm busy convincing myself not to crawl over this table like a stripper and straddle him.

"Morning. I didn't see your car."

The usual smirk arises, his fingers tapping on the table. "Did you see the black pick-up truck?"

I nod, my heart skipping a beat for what day two in the win-over-Ava-game might bring.

"It's mine. I traded in the 'stang. I'm not up to pick-up level yet, but hey, if you want more kids, a car seat could fit next to Toby in the back so I figure we have a least a couple years with this one." His lips curl up further, and eventually he loses the battle, chuckling.

I try and keep the smile from spreading across my face. "What if I had triplets?"

"Then we'll get a Suburban." He points to himself. "See, not even a stutter."

I nod. "Good to know."

"Food for thought, right? Kids and marriage don't scare me, as long as you're part of the equation."

He slides the stool out and disappears back into the storage room.

Day Three

MY FRONT DOOR SHUTS BEHIND ME, BUT MY FEET DON'T MAKE the daily trek to Mad Batter because Dane is parked in my building's lot, leaning back on the front of his truck.

He pushes off and walks toward me, a coffee from Steaming Hotties in his hands.

I tentatively take it from him.

He circles around and holds out his arm for me to take like he's a debonair gentleman escorting me into a ball. "Let's go shopping."

"What?" I loop my arm through his.

"Shopping. You need some things so we're going to take a day trip."

"What day is this again?" I ask, falling into step with him.

"Day three. Why? Have I already convinced you that I'm not acting out of fear?" His footsteps stop and he looks down at me.

"I'm just curious, how long you'll be able to keep this up for."

He leans closer, opening the passenger side door for me. "Until you accept my apology."

"I already accepted your apology." I slide into the front seat of his new vehicle.

He shakes his head. "Not really. Not if you're not willing to take me back."

He shuts the door, circles around the front of the vehicle and hops in next to me.

"I promise, no griping, no arguing, and no whining. I will willingly carry things, haul things, and help with decision making all day." He holds out his pinky. "Pinky swear."

My pinky clasps onto his and the butterflies in my stomach start flapping their wings frantically at his touch.

"We'll see."

"You can't break me, Ava Pearson."

He was right, the entire day he was at my side, and by the time we headed back to Climax Cove, the truck bed was full of new supplies for the bakery.

Day Four

THE BAKERY IS COMING ALONG AND SINCE I MISSED YESTERDAY, I'm eager to see how far the crew has come on the rebuild. I still need to do a big meal or something to thank all these people for helping me without any pay or complaints.

I'm about to cross the street when Dane approaches and puts his arm over my shoulder. I'd be lying if I said we hadn't touched during our day trip yesterday. No smooching or hand holding, but our limbs brushed occasionally and every time they did, I thought I'd have to call the fire department to hose me down.

"What are you doing?" I ask.

He continues to lead me away from the bakery and right to the doors of his bar.

"A few customers have been jonesing for your cupcakes."

We walk through the bar to the back kitchen. On the counter rests flour, sugar, and an array of baking ingredients.

"This is yours for the day. I've closed the grill until dinner." He winks and then turns on his heels, but peeks his head back into the room. "Of course, if you feel obliged to pay me back, I'll gladly take payment in peanut butter and chocolate cupcakes."

He chuckles and I hear the door shut behind him, leaving me alone in the bar.

A few minutes later Charlie comes in and pulls up a stool from the corner beside me.

"Still playing that hard to get role, huh?" she asks.

"I'm not playing anything."

I look around for an apron, finding a section on the back wall where I see some.

I pick one up and put it over my head.

Charlie starts laughing and shaking her head.

"What?"

She points to the apron and my eyes venture down. On the front it reads, 'I <3 Dane' under it.

"He's pulling out all the stops." She shakes her head. "If I were you, I'd keep the whole chase-me thing up to see what else he'll come up with."

She vanishes into the bar and I'm left alone in a foreign kitchen with my thoughts about Dane. I'm not purposely playing a game of cat and mouse with him, but putting my heart out there in case he really isn't in this is hard. What if he gets scared and changes his mind?

It's in his kitchen that I realize why Dane gave me a space to bake. It wasn't because the town wanted my cupcakes, it's because my best thinking happens when I'm mixing and baking and creating. One thing is clear, he's weaseling his way back in and I now know I want nothing more than for him to prove me wrong.

Day Five

I roll over and when I go to check the time I see that I have a bunch of notifications on Instagram.

That's weird.

I open the app and that's when I see that Dane has tagged me in roughly twenty pictures of the two of us from our shopping excursion the other day. His profile picture is of me at his house staring out at the ocean. I'm not even sure when he took it, but I clearly didn't know he was capturing the moment.

The hashtag with the picture is #needmorenights-likethis.

I go to his photos and see he's erased any pictures of him with other women. I'm the only female on his page besides his mother and one of Charlie flipping him off.

He's definitely in it to win it.

Day Six

I haven't even had breakfast when there's a knock on

my door. Charlie went for a run this morning and Cat is at Marcus' of course, so I open the door, finding Toby in pants and a t-shirt.

"I'm rafting the class three today." He jumps into my house and I spot Dane just stepping out of his truck.

"Oh, that's great!"

"Get your stuff." He looks around my apartment. "This is where you live?"

"Yeah, what do you think?"

"It's small." His gaze continues to roam around.

"Well, Miss Cat isn't here a lot, so it's just Charlie and I most of the time."

I'm still holding the door open when Dane approaches.

He's in shorts and a hoodie with a t-shirt underneath, his sunglasses resting on top of his head.

"Did you convince her?" he asks Toby.

"You're letting him raft another class three, huh?"

"I promised. And I never break a promise." He winks, walks in, and sits on my couch.

Toby takes the spot next to him, the two of them propping their feet on my coffee table.

"Has no one taught you any manners? I didn't ask you to come in, nor is it ever okay to put your feet on someone's table."

I shut the door and smack both their feet. They plop down on the floor.

"See, that's why we need a woman in our life," Toby says.

"You've upped your game to include Toby?" I cross my arms over my chest and cock a hip out to the side.

He shrugs and links his fingers behind his head. "Hey, all's fair in love and war, right?" He pauses for a second, his gaze roaming up and down my body taking in my yoga pants and tight tank top. "Go get dressed."

"Both of you need to say please."

"Please," they each say simultaneously in such sweet voices.

"I can't be gone all day."

"Yay! Thanks, Miss Ava." Toby jumps up from the couch.

A half hour later, we're at the rafting place and surprise surprise—they have reservations for three. Once our life-jackets are on and we're about to get in the raft, Dane pulls his camera out and positions it like he's about to take a selfie.

"Come on," he calls us over and Toby and I huddle together with him while he snaps the picture.

A second later, my phone vibrates and I pull it out, looking through the plastic bag to find another Instagram notification.

Dane's posted the picture he just took. Reading the caption #familyday makes my heart warm and go pitter-patter.

Day Seven (actually night of day six)

"Do you mind if we stop at the bar really quick?" Dane asks after we spent majority of the day on the rapids.

Toby's asleep in the back of the truck after nailing the class three rafting again.

"Sure."

When we arrive, every parking spot is taken, leaving Dane to go to the back and park in the alley where the deliveries usually come through. He stops the truck and pulls out the keys, glancing back to Toby who's now steadily breathing.

Turning in his seat, he reaches for my hand and for the first time since our argument, I don't pull away.

"Ava, tonight marks the end of day six. I know I promised I'd win you back in seven days, but I only have one more thing up my sleeve. I thought long and hard about what you said the night of the fire. Was I acting out of fear? Probably."

My heart sinks.

"But if I didn't love you, I'd have nothing to fear. I can't help but want to protect the ones I love."

My sinking heart has been tossed a life raft and wants desperately to latch on to it.

"I realized that most my life, I've lived in fear without knowing it. When I told you I couldn't give you what you wanted, *that* was out of fear...fear of not being good enough, fear of hurting you, fear of hurting Toby, fear of me being hurt. Even without the fire happening, I'd have realized how much I want to take a chance with you to develop something more than what we had. Truth is, we weren't friends-with-benefits, we *were* boyfriend and girl-friend. If you want more time, I'll wait because I was living my life on a carousel, just going round and round. Our life together might be more like a roller coaster, but I want you next to me on it. Otherwise the ride isn't going to be any fun."

He leans forward and presses a kiss on my cheek and I can't deny that it feels so right to have his lips on me again.

"I promise to never hurt you again."

He opens the truck door, tucking his keys in his pocket.

"This is my last attempt to win you over."

I could probably tell him he's already won me over, but making him suffer a couple extra minutes until I see what he has planned inside doesn't seem like that bad of an idea.

He nudges Toby awake, carrying him in his arms as we walk through the back door.

I hear Charlie over a microphone and quirk my eyebrows to Dane who only wears that smile I've wanted to kiss off him for the past few days.

He stops us at the opening of the hallway into the bar. Everyone from town is sitting around, eating the cupcakes I made yesterday. There's a giant banner on the window that says, 'Save the Mad Batter'.

Charlie spots us and smiles, placing the microphone down and coming toward us. "Welcome."

"What is this?" I ask.

Then Cat grabs the microphone. "Okay, the first auction is a two-night stay at one of Garrett Shaw's log cabins. Let's start the bidding at one hundred."

A bunch of hands rise in the air.

"Oh, hold on." Charlie's hand touches my arm.

"You going for it?" Dane asks, and Charlie nods, her hand up in the air.

"One thousand dollars," she says.

The room gasps, everyone looking over their shoulders at her. Most of the crowd is smiling, but I can't help but zoom in on the one face that is not. Garrett's.

Cat slams down the gavel before anyone can up the bid. "Sold to the lovely Charlotte Rose for one thousand dollars." Cat smiles from ear to ear.

Garrett slides by the table and Cat, his footsteps heavy on the floor as he makes his way over to Charlie. Without a word, he grabs her elbow and escorts her down the hallway.

"Settle, Garrett," Dane says after them, but before either of us can see what's happening, Cat's announcing our presence.

"Our guest of honor has arrived!" All eyes are on us.

"What is this?" I ask Dane a second time.

"It's a fundraiser. For you." He knocks his free shoulder with mine since somehow Toby's still asleep on his other shoulder.

"You did this?" Tears well up in my eyes.

He nods, shifting Toby's weight in his arms.

"Here." His dad comes and takes Toby from Dane and sits back down.

"Okay, they're busy," Cat says over the mic. "Let's do our second auction. A moonlight cruise on a yacht from Marcus Kent. Let's start the bidding at one hundred." Again, hands go up in the air and as the people are busy bidding, I'm busy looking at my unlikely hero.

"So, did this seal the deal?" Dane asks, stepping closer to me.

"As long as we can make one thing clear."

"What's that?" he asks with a smirk.

"We might be monogamous, but the bedroom is always more like thirty-one flavors."

"You mean you don't want me to lose my dirty mouth?"

I shake my head. "No, I love my dirty talker. But you can't lose the 'you're beautiful' and 'I love you's' either. Well, what do you say?"

"I promise to mix it up." He holds his pinky out. "Pinky swear."

I clasp my pinky with his, pulling him forward until we're chest-to-chest and I'm once again in his arms.

"Now kiss me."

EPILOGUE

Two Years Later

Talk about using all my connections to pull this off. It all goes to show how awesome Climax Cove and their residents are.

This has been a year in the making, considering the shrubs were planted last spring to grow into a maze this summer. A town silently pushed toward an Alice in Wonderland theme festival night without thinking twice about it. A girlfriend I somehow managed to keep oblivious.

"Can we go through the maze?" Toby asks next to me.

Do you know how hard it is to get a ten-year-old boy to sound excited to go through an Alice In Wonderland maze? For future reference, it takes a twenty-dollar bill and a new video game.

"You want to go?" Ava looks down skeptically at him.

Out of all the hoops I went through to get her to believe this act, I should've known this is the part she'd question.

"I think he's throwing you a bone," I lean close, whisper in her ear, and kiss her neck.

The distraction works. She places her arm around Toby, who's catching up to her height wise and the two of them enter through the giant red heart balloon archway.

I follow behind, pretending to be checking the score of the Giants game when in fact, I'm busy texting Cat and Charlie to make sure everything is a go once we get through this maze.

"Who did the maze?" Ava asks.

Toby's now away from Ava since a few his friends followed us in.

So much for his video game, the kid can play last year's Madden now.

I link my hand with Ava's. "I don't know. Want to find a spot to make-out?" My fingers tighten around hers, and she looks at me and smiles.

"I wouldn't want to embarrass Toby." Her words say one thing, but the spark of lust in her eyes says another.

If it were any other day, any other time, I'd corner her between two bushes and lick her own perfectly manicured bush. But today is about so much more than that.

"This way." I purposely go a different way from Toby and his friends.

"A dead end?" Her hand slides down my front until she cups my package.

"I actually hadn't planned that, but now..." Her thumb runs up and down my now bulging shaft. Reluctantly I reach down and stop her hand from moving. "Damn, that feels good, but let's get out of here and then I can take you home. Remember, Toby is sleeping over at Carter's tonight."

I pull her into my chest, and she nuzzles into it like she

always does. The fruity smell of her shampoo never fails to calm me.

"Let's go."

My hand glides down her arm until her hand is tucked in mine once more.

"What's the rush?" Her footsteps falter, but she stays in step, eventually coming to my side.

"Just eager to have you in our bed."

"I do like the sound of that."

We navigate the maze and I allow her to take a wrong turn here and there since I practically mapped the whole thing out so that where we end up is right on the water. What seems like a lifetime later and with my heart pounding in my chest, we're one turn away from the exit.

She takes the lead and I watch her round the corner.

"Oh, a tea party!" She glances back to me and then forward again. "Come on."

If everything is on cue, Lily should be approaching her in a costume.

"Hey, Lily," she says, bending down and grabbing the little girl's hands.

Ava glances back to me and nods for me to follow.

I round the corner she did, emerging to see that Cat and Charlie did a bang-up job. Tables are filled with guests. They've covered the cement walkway with black and white checkered flooring. The tablecloths are all different colors paired with an array of colored chairs and huge fake flowers hung all around.

I hang back, letting Ava take in the moment, soak up her surroundings and say her hellos. After awhile she turns back my way and holds a hand out for me to join her. I don't think she's clued into what this is all about yet.

Toby intercedes like he's supposed to and escorts her to

a chair in the middle of the room. A big cushy chair you'd see a queen sit in.

Her gaze roams over to me and I see it then. The moment she realizes what this is. The lottery-winning smile on her face tells me I'm not about to make a fool of myself.

All our friends and family who are in on this moment—whether they've known for a long time or just found out when they arrived this evening—circle behind around us.

"Ava." I clench and open my fists a few times to work out the nerves I can't seem to shake.

"Yes?" She bites her lip, waiting for me to pull out the box. Waiting for the magic four words.

"I could've taken you to a Giants game and flashed it on the jumbotron. I could've asked you while we watched the sunset on the dock the other night. There are a lot of ways I thought about proposing to you, but the fact that you love Alice in Wonderland isn't the reason why I chose this way. There have been perfect moments this past year where I could've asked you and it would have been wonderful. Never in my life did I think I'd be patient enough to wait and make sure you had the perfect proposal, but I did because that's what you deserve. Two years ago, I got lost in your wonderland and the last thing I want is a map to find my way out." I fall to my knee and her hands move to her lips immediately as she sucks in a breath.

"Will you do me a favor and tolerate me for another fifty or so years?"

She slides off the chair and onto her knees until we're chest to chest. "Yes," she whispers, her arms wrapping around my neck. But I stop her, holding her left ring finger until I can slip on the ring I got her.

She smashes into my body until I lose my balance and

fall to the ground. Sprinkling kisses all over my face, she quickly looks down at me, worry teasing her brow.

"Is this because you love my cupcakes?"

"Well..."

She shakes her head. "Peanut butter and chocolate cupcakes everyday for the rest of your life?"

"You know better than that. I need variety so mix that up with some vanilla, salted caramel, and unicorn rainbow ones and we're good."

She giggles and sits up, pulling me up by my hand. "Deal."

"I love you," I say to her, bending down to kiss her lips.

"Not nearly as much as I love you."

I'll let her go on thinking that, but the truth is that Ava fills my life up in a way I didn't think was possible. I was lost before she came around. I just didn't know it until she found me.

The End

COCKAMAMIE UNICORN RAMBLINGS

In the back of Real Deal's Cockamamie Unicorn Ramblings we told you how Piper tapped into her cougar side, spying on all the hot camp counselors while picking up her kids, which spurred the entire Single Dads Club series. So, let's talk Dane ...

ORIGINALLY, WE HAD DECIDED THAT EACH BOOK IN THIS SERIES would happen during the same time frame. Each girl would be a camp counselor of the single dad's child. Then we realized, well, that would be slightly boring, but we wrote ourselves in a corner with Real Deal. Mostly, because as Rayne writes she detours off route and let's her mind wander. So, suddenly we had Ava coming in the morning disheveled from a night of sex and then we had her go off on Dane because of Toby at the camp. Which meant they had to have slept together twice instead of once which put a crimp in our original plot. I'm sure there will be twists and turns to Sexy Beast due to where we put Charlie and Garrett in Dirty Talker. Surprises await.

. . .

Here are some things we really didn't plot out...

Ava opening up a cupcake shop wasn't originally planned until Cat walked in one day and Ava was in the kitchen making cupcakes. Even then we had no reason why she was baking and trying to perfect recipes. However, once we got a feel more of her character, we purposely did have Charlie bring the cupcakes in and have Dane be obsessed with them.

Originally, Ava and Dane were going to be sneaking around behind everyone's back during the camp season, but after we decided we needed more than another camp counselor and single dad story, we pushed their story up to right after camp got out. Plus, it was nice to see Cat, Marcus, and Lily living out their HEA.

Charlie wasn't planned to have such a big role in Dirty Talker, but she challenged Dane in a way we loved and it wasn't until after we finished writing the book did we realize, how is she always at the bar when she's actually a counselor ... "Hello Corner, we're Rayne and Piper, how do we get ourselves out of here?"

We weren't originally going to tell you all that Garrett's wife passed away, but we gave you that little nugget early because we're nice like that. lol Although, we didn't give you all the details on how and when. We have to keep you wanting more, right?

THE SAME AS WITH REAL DEAL, WITHOUT THE HELP OF THE following people in our corner we wouldn't have released this book.

Letitia from RBA Designs for the amazing covers and for putting up with how nitpicky we can be.

Ellie from Love N Books for line editing. You're new nickname is Speedy Ellie.

Shawna from Behind the Writer for her eagle eye proof-reading skills and working through migraines to get this one done for us.

Enticing Journey Book Promotions for their organization and helping us out with all the Single Dads Club Series.

All the bloggers who carved out time to promote us and/or read and review the book.

Michelle New for yet another set of awesome graphics.

Our first readers of a really shitty, unedited copy—Heather and Angela.

Christine from Type A Formatting for such a pretty paperback.

All our early ARC readers, first for wanting to read our stuff early and for posting their reviews.

And of course, all our unicorns. <3 Your enthusiasm for our work knows no bounds. From sharing unicorn para-phernalia in our reader group and shouting from the rooftops to anyone who will listen that they should read our work. The best part of this new endeavor has been having you in our corner!

Can't wait for you to read Garrett's story. Don't forget we

have one more couple from Modern Love that you've yet to hear from. Did you do the math? That's right, where are Lennon and Jasper six years later???

> *xo,*
> *Piper & Rayne*

ABOUT THE AUTHOR

Piper Rayne, or Piper and Rayne, whichever you prefer because we're not one author, we're two. Yep, you get two USA Today Bestselling authors for the price of one. Our goal is to bring you romance stories that have "Heart-warming Humor With a Side of Sizzle" (okay...you caught us, that's our tagline). A little about us... We both have kindle's full of one-clickable books. We're both married to husbands who drive us to drink. We're both chauffeurs to our kids. Most of all, we love hot heroes and quirky heroines that make us laugh, and we hope you do, too.

Goodreads
Facebook
Instagram
Pinterest
Bookbub
www.piperrayne.com

Join our newsletter and get 2 FREE BOOKS!
http://bit.ly/2tsNcpP

Be one of our UNICORNS and join our Facebook group!

ALSO BY PIPER RAYNE

The Modern Love World

Charmed by the Bartender

Hooked by the Boxer

Mad about the Banker

The Single Dad's Club

Real Deal

Dirty Talker

Sexy Beast

Hollywood Hearts

Mister Mom

Animal Attraction

Domestic Bliss

Bedroom Games

Cold as Ice

On Thin Ice

Break the Ice

Box Set

Charity Case

Manic Monday

Afternoon Delight

Happy Hour

Blue Collar Brothers

Flirting with Fire

Crushing on the Cop

Engaged to the EMT

The Baileys

Lessons from a One-Night Stand

Advice from a Jilted Bride

Birth of a Baby Daddy

Made in United States
North Haven, CT
26 April 2022

18570920R00159